Sherlock Holmes and
The Murder At Lodore Falls

and other minor tales

As related from the case notes of
Dr. John H. Watson, M.D.

Charlotte Smith

Paperback ISBN 9781780921747
ePub ISBN 9781780921754
PDF ISBN 9781780921761

Published in the UK by MX Publishing
335 Princess Park Manor, Royal Drive, London, N11 3GX
www.mxpublishing.com

Cover design by
www.staunch.com

Acknowledgements

Firstly to my parents, whom I love so very much, and especially my Mother, who I miss more than words will ever convey. I have a number of other people to thank. My editor Izabella Balakirsky, for her dedication and hard work in reviewing this book. Many thanks to CFP for her insight, encouragement, and stylistic suggestions. I would also like to extend my heartfelt thanks to my friends who have supported me over the years in my love of writing and whose enthusiasm has kept me going. Additionally, I can't not mention my senior school English teacher Margaret Kay. A lovely lady who nurtured my creativity in writing and performing on stage. She is very much missed. I am sure she would be thrilled to see this publication.

Contents

Prologue

August 1896

Dr Watson buried his face in his hands with the shocking realisation that Sherlock Holmes had fallen into the watery abyss with Professor Moriarty. Watson felt his world shatter—his closest friend was dead. His chest tightened until he could hardly breathe and tears were stinging his eyes. From the depths of the Reichenbach Falls, a pair of glowing red eyes stared at Watson, claw-like hands reached out towards his face, and chilling laughter reverberated round the ravine. Watson screamed. The horrific vision vanished, and Watson suddenly woke with a jolt, drenched in sweat. He opened his eyes, and the familiar sight of his Baker Street room greeted him. He was home and safe. With a sigh, Watson ran a hand over his face and through his hair. His nightmares were getting worse.

Putting on his dressing gown, he made his way down the stairs to the sitting room he shared with Holmes and looked at the drawing of the waterfall that hung above the fireplace. A strong sense of foreboding grew within him. Watson steadied himself against the fireplace. He took a cigarette from the mantelpiece, lit it, threw the match into the grate and headed toward the window, inhaling the smoke deeply. Watching the start of a new day, he was thankful that Holmes was not dead but with him in Baker Street. *So why am I having these nightmares?* Watson knew Holmes had become increasingly worried by his disturbed sleep. Watson could no longer continue to make excuses and would have to share his nightmares with his friend. At least he knew Holmes would help him. They would get through this together, as they had so many times before.

Had Watson known of the horror to come, he would have screamed even louder in his nightmares.

Chapter One

A Year Earlier—August 1895
Matthew Crowther was a worried man. His civil engineering business, situated in the beautiful Lakeland countryside, was flourishing and he had just gone into partnership with his cousin Brett Sullivan and his friend Danny Peterson. Both Danny and Brett had been recently invalided out of the Army after fighting in Afghanistan. Danny was recovered from his injuries but would never again have the use of his left eye. Brett had been more severely injured, and had almost died in the field hospital from a wound infection. His physical recovery was much slower than Danny's and he still carried very raw mental scars. Matthew's offering Brett and Danny the partnership had given them both a welcome distraction from the horrors of war. But it was not the partnership or Brett's health that was troubling Matthew.

A year earlier, he had accepted the help of some creditors to finance his company's development of a new explosive material that would make the excavation and demolition work much easier. But it was not long after that the first threats came. At first, it was just trivial incidents such as the office window being broken in what Matthew had thought was an accident, but things gradually grew more menacing and now Matthew Crowther stared down at the latest malicious letter received in the post that morning. It was a direct threat to his life. The demand was simple--hand over the formula for the explosive or face the consequences. His hands shaking, Matthew crumpled up the letter into a ball.

"My God, what have I got myself into?!" Matthew muttered.

He looked down at his pocket watch, a birthday present he had received from his cousin the previous month. It was an 18-carat gold pocket watch repeater, inscribed *Happy Birthday Matt from Brett.* Matthew smiled. He and Brett had been more like brothers than cousins. He knew his life was in danger now but he was not going to drag Brett and Danny into this awful situation; he had to face it alone. But he was damned if he was going to let the formula fall into the wrong hands. Matthew opened his desk drawer and pulled out a blue envelope. Inside the envelope was a small piece of paper. Matthew folded it up into an even smaller size, opened up the back of his pocket watch, and inserted the folded paper inside the watch. He placed the watch in a cardboard box, sealed the box, and wrote his cousin's address on the top. He got up from his desk, grabbed his coat and walking stick, and walked out of his office to greet the receptionist, who was quietly filing away papers.

"Sally, I am going for a walk, can you please ensure this parcel is posted?"

Sally, a petite girl no more than twenty-two years old with brown curly hair, replied,

"Yes, Mr Crowther, will there be anything else, sir?"

Matthew shook his head.

"No, Sally, I'll be out for a few hours, so if anyone comes looking for me I won't be in, but if Matthew or Danny asks tell them I have gone to the Lodore Falls." [1]

Matthew left the office and was soon walking in the crisp winter morning air. It had snowed overnight and a light dusting of snow blanketed the countryside. He wrapped his heavy coat round him to keep out the chill air. After an hour's walk, Matthew found himself standing at the foot of Lodore Falls. He felt strangely calm and at peace with himself. When they were children, he used to come here often with Brett and had known the area well. Matthew lit a cigar and contemplated. Here, he could leave behind all his troubles and threats and simply enjoy the solitude of this beautiful spot with the sound of gushing water below.

Suddenly, he was grabbed from behind, wrestled to the floor, and savagely kicked in the ribs.

"Are you going to tell us where the formula is or do I have to break every bone in your body?" said a menacing rough voice.

Matthew hardly had time to regain his composure and was clutching his side from the assault on his ribs. He breathed in hard and immediately regretted it as he felt a sharp pain protesting from his side. Matthew looked up

---

[1] Lodore Falls is located in Derwentwater, Keswick, in the Lake District, UK.

to face his attacker. Matthew's eyes locked onto a chisel-faced man; his face sported black stubble and was etched by years of weathering by the wind. His brown eyes had an evil allure about them and Matthew grew frightened.

"Who are you, and what is the meaning of this assault?"

The chisel-faced man grabbed the lapels of Matthew's coat with his left hand and raised his right fist, ready to strike a blow.

"Never mind who I am, I want that formula and if you value your life you will tell me where it is or I will break your neck."

Matthew knew this was going to end badly, realising the months of threats and intimidation had built up to this moment. He laughed and replied defiantly,

"I don't have any formulas with me and if I did I would certainly not put them in your hands or the hands of whoever else is threatening me. You have no power over me, I defy you!"

With a snarl of contempt, the chisel-faced man smashed his fist into Matthew's jaw, sending him sprawling down onto the rocky path. Strong hands encircled his neck and he felt them slowly and painfully choking the air out of him.

"You will tell me now where the formula is."

Matthew struggled against the brute force of his attacker and spluttered, "Go to hell!"

Matthew's attacker lashed out in full blind fury and Matthew staggered back, dangerously close to the edge of the ravine. He was precariously balanced on the edge between safety and a long drop below, and his feet were slipping. The attacker again had his burly hands around Matthew's neck and gave a malevolent grin, "You don't mess with the James Gang, this is your last chance, tell me or die."

Matthew struck out hopelessly at his formidable attacker, who responded with a powerful punch to his mid section. Matthew lost his footing and went flying into the ravine below. He cried out, knowing he was falling to his death. His head hit the jagged rocks below with a sickening crunch. A crimson pool started forming, mixing with the watery current. Matthew's green eyes grew wide open in terror, and then the spark in his eyes faded and died.

Chapter Two

 Brett Sullivan was in the throes of a recurring nightmare, except this nightmare had been all too real only a year ago. He was in the midst of a savage battle in the mountains of South Africa. Cut off from the rest of his unit, he was facing twenty or more tribesmen armed with guns and knives. They were closing in on him, and Brett only had his revolver with just two bullets left in it. Before he could use it, he felt a sharp pain as a bullet hit him in the side, and again as another bullet hit him in the leg. The tribesmen were moving in for the kill and Brett screamed, lashed out, and then felt a knife dig deep into his back. He was going to die. He struggled, finding it difficult to breathe. Blackness was descending on him. Suddenly there was banging and shouting, which jolted Brett awake from his nightmare. He caught his breath and rubbed his tired eyes. The banging at his door continued and Brett became annoyed.

"All right, all right, I'm coming!" he shouted angrily.

Brett rose from his bed, still moving painfully. With the aid of his cane, he slowly walked to the front door, ready to give whoever was banging on it a piece of his mind. He was shocked to find Danny standing there with Inspector Roche from the Keswick Police Station.

"Danny, what's the matter? What are the police doing here-- has there been a break-in at the office?"

8

Danny looked distraught and somber.

"Brett, can we come in? I would prefer to discuss this inside rather than in the middle of the street."
Brett caught his breath, suddenly realising that this was far more serious than a break-in. He began to fear the worst as he guided his unexpected guests into his living room.

"Danny...has something happened to Matthew?"

Inspector Roche broke in before Danny could respond, "Sir, I regret to inform you that your cousin was found dead this morning at the bottom of Lodore Falls."

Brett felt his knees buckle and the room swirl round him. Danny reached forward and guided Brett to a nearby chair.
Brett bowed his head. After a short while, he looked up and his blue eyes fixed upon the Inspector.

"What happened?" asked Brett, his voice thick with grief.

"Well, sir, we found him at the bottom of the waterfall. It looks like he slipped and fell. Everything points to a terrible accident. My condolences for your loss, sir."

Brett nodded and stood up weakly, leaning on Danny.

"I want to go to the Lodore Falls to see for myself."

Danny protested, "Brett, you can't go up there! You simply haven't the strength for such a strenuous walk."

Brett shot Danny a look, his blue eyes blazing with barely repressed anger, then softening as he realised Danny only had his best interests at heart.
"Danny, I have to go and see this for myself. Matt was more like a brother to me than my cousin, just as you are to me, my dear fellow."

Danny nodded; they had been through a great deal together back in South Africa and Danny would not abandon Brett now in this hour of need.

"I understand, my friend, but I'm coming with you."

Brett smiled faintly. "Thank you Danny, I knew you would, and I'm grateful for your support."

The three of them left the house and made their way to the Lodore Falls. On the way to the falls, Brett had struggled with the terrain and leant heavily on Danny, who was more than half carrying him. Together, they stared down into the waterfall, unprepared for the grisly sight that awaited them. The body of Matthew Crowther was still lying sprawled in the ravine. Brett could not restrain a cry. He closed his eyes, shutting out the scene below. He had seen death many times in South Africa, but this was his cousin and close friend.

Inspector Roche angrily barked an order to his officers to cover up the body and apologised, "I'm sorry you saw that, I had expected the body to have been removed by now."

Danny waved the inspector off, indicating the need for both him and Brett to be alone. They stood quietly supporting each other and stared into the countryside, both lost in their thoughts.
At long last, Brett motioned that he wanted to leave, and they slowly made their way back down to the small town. After they arrived at Brett's house, the Inspector made his farewells and discreetly left. Danny wanted to stay to support his friend but Brett gripped Danny's shoulder and said,

"No, please leave me now. Thank you for being at my side but I need time to myself".

Danny began to object but Brett looked at him with a resolute glint in his eyes. Danny knew what that look meant; it was a warning that Brett had drawn a line and Danny should not attempt to cross it. Danny conceded.

"All right, I'll go, but if you need anything, anything at all, just call for me and I'll be here."

Brett drew Danny into a bear hug and gripped his shoulder once more. "Thanks, Danny, I appreciate that."

Brett smiled at his trusty former Sergeant and turned to close the front door behind him. He barely managed to make it to his sitting room before he could no longer hold back his tears. He dashed them away angrily and felt his knees buckle as he collapsed to the floor, narrowly missing his couch. He reached up for the edge of his couch, stretching his arm to pull himself up, and his hand touched a box. Someone must have left it for him whilst he was out at Lodore Falls. His curiosity aroused, he opened the parcel and found a pocket watch inside—the watch he'd given Matthew for his birthday. Why would Matthew send him this watch? Brett opened the front of the watch and then the back. It appeared to be in working order, but then Brett noticed a small piece of folded paper inside. Brett unfolded the paper and his eyes widened in horror at what was written on it. His cousin had not died accidentally. He had been murdered. Brett gripped the watch firmly in his hands and his face suddenly darkened. In that moment he swore he would hunt down whoever was responsible for his cousin's death and would not rest till justice had been served.

Chapter Three

Sherlock Holmes had lain awake in his bed for the last fifteen minutes. He heard Dr Watson moving around in the sitting room and frowned. Looking at his pocket watch, Holmes saw it was only five o'clock in the morning. Watson was clearly still troubled by his disturbed sleep and it pained Holmes to see his friend suffer. Holmes got out of bed and put on his dressing gown, determined to resolve whatever was troubling his friend. Walking into the sitting room, he saw Watson leaning against the window pane smoking a cigarette. Much to Holmes's surprise, he looked more tired than he had permitted Holmes to see.

"Watson, my dear friend, what is ailing you? You have spent the last few nights pacing your room and now you are up at this early hour looking more tired than I've seen you in a long time. Pray tell me what is wrong?"

In a futile attempt to distract himself, Watson had been looking out the window. He observed man walking down Baker Street. The man's gait was unsteady; *probably drunk*, thought Watson.
Watson turned to face Holmes and clearly saw the concern in his face. Realising he would have to tell Holmes the truth, Watson sat down wearily in his chair.

"Holmes, I'm sure you know I haven't slept well lately. I had hoped this would resolve itself by now, but I'm still having nightmares--I can't seem to make them go away," Watson's voice was trembling with exhaustion.

Holmes moved to Watson's side, placed a hand on Watson's shoulder and said softly,
"Perhaps it would help if you described what the nightmares are about, John."

Watson looked up in surprise at Holmes's rare use of his first name. It was an indication of how worried Holmes really was.
"Holmes, I keep dreaming about the Reichenbach Falls and of losing you in that awful abyss and I..."

Watson hid his face in his hands, trying to conceal the pain he felt.

"Oh my dear friend," said Holmes. "I am so very sorry for the pain I have caused you, but I am here now and the danger from Professor Moriarty is past." Holmes gripped Watson's arms in an attempt to reassure him. Watson looked up and returned the gesture.

"Holmes, there is more..."

But before Watson could complete his sentence, they were both startled by Mrs Hudson's scream from downstairs. As one, they both leapt up and raced for the door. Holmes got there first and flung it open. Mrs Hudson stood at the open front door and a figure dressed in a heavy coat covered in mud and straw was slumped in the hallway next to her. Holmes raced down the stairs and knelt down beside the slumped form. He gently turned over the inert body to reveal a blond-haired man with a nasty-looking gash to his forehead. Holmes turned to Watson, who was comforting the shocked Mrs Hudson.

"Watson, I think this man needs your medical services." Watson knelt down next to Holmes and began his examination. "He is still breathing, Holmes, and he has a pulse, but it is weak."

Watson continued his examination, feeling down the man's torso in a methodical manner, then doing the same to his arms and legs.

"He appears to have sustained a cracked rib and injured his shoulder. I'll need to examine him further. Can you help me carry him upstairs?"

Holmes nodded, wrapping his arms round the man's waist to lift him up from the floor.

The movement up the stairs stirred the man to partial consciousness. Just as Holmes and Watson reached the sitting room and were settling the injured man down on the settee, he tried to speak groggily,

"Danny?...help me....trying to kill me...must find help...Danny?"

With a groan, the injured man lapsed back into unconsciousness.

Watson had grabbed his medical bag and was already working on his patient, his own troubles cast aside as his professional training took over.

Sitting quietly opposite Watson, Holmes watched him work. He admired the doctor for his ability to look after others when he was in need of help himself. Holmes pressed a finger to his lips, his eyebrows furrowed deep in thought.
Who was this man? What danger was he in and who was trying to kill him?
Holmes's eyes shone in anticipation of a new case before him. Watson completed his assessment and treatment of his patient and turned to Holmes.

"He's badly hurt, Holmes; he is severely concussed and has definitely cracked a rib. His left shoulder is badly bruised, pointing to a heavy fall, and there is renewed aggravation to earlier injuries which will cause him some considerable discomfort once he awakens."

"Well, Watson, it seems we have a case on our hands but we won't know more until he comes round. You look tired; why don't you get some rest while I watch your patient?"

Watson began to object but bit back his retort.
Holmes is right, I do feel tired; an hour's sleep would do me good, thought Watson as he stood up, massaging the kinks from his lower back.

"Thank you, Holmes, I could do with some rest. I'll join you again in an hour."

The game's afoot, thought Holmes as he lay back in his chair and kept vigil over the sleeping form opposite. Little did Holmes know how dangerous the game would become for both himself and Watson.

Chapter Four

Brett Sullivan awoke to the strong smell of tobacco. He slowly opened his eyes and found himself staring at the ceiling. His head was throbbing badly and he raised his hand to massage his temple. As the realisation of what had happened to him came flooding back, he tried to sit up but felt strong hands holding him down.

"Steady man, Dr Watson will never forgive me if I do not prevent you from undoing his ministrations!"

Brett focused on the person who was speaking to him. He saw a thin but athletically built man bending over him. His grey eyes betrayed his concern but his voice had a ring of authority that told Brett he was not going anywhere. Brett's attempt to move had exhausted him and he dropped back against the couch, feeling his limbs going slack. He watched the tall lean stranger sit back in the chair opposite him. Brett swallowed and cleared his throat, desperately trying to focus.

"Who are you? Where am I? And where is Danny?" asked Brett, anxious for some answers.

Holmes was about to reply when the door to the sitting room opened and Dr Watson came in.

"Ah, Watson, you came just in time, your patient has awakened but a moment ago."

Dr Watson approached Brett, casting a clinical eye over him.

"My name is Dr Watson, and this is Sherlock Holmes," said Watson who pointed to Sherlock Holmes and was now checking Brett's pulse.

"We found you unconscious in our hallway. How do you feel?"
Brett rubbed his temples once more and looked at Watson.

"Like wild horses have trodden all over me."

Brett chuckled briefly and continued,

"Then again I *was* ridden over by horses—the cabman was racing his carriage so quickly I barely had time to clear out of the way."

Holmes sat up in his chair, fingertips steepled and eyes alight.

"You're saying someone tried to run you over, Mr--?"

Brett nodded and immediately regretted it as the throbbing began once more.

"Mr Sullivan, sir, Brett Sullivan. Not 'someone', but people, Mr Holmes."
Holmes leant forward and said softly,

"I think you had better start from the beginning, Mr Sullivan. I should like to hear more of this."

Brett looked quizzically at Holmes, then at Dr Watson, who sought to reassure him.

"Mr Holmes is a consulting detective. He investigates criminal matters and may be able to help you."

"Mr Holmes," said Brett, "I mean no offence, but the Keswick police couldn't help me and no one can protect me from the violent gang who wants me dead..."

Holmes raised his hand and halted Brett.

"Mr Sullivan, let me be the judge of that. I enjoy a challenge, and I have already observed much about you. I know you are a man with a military background, having observed the service ring on your left middle finger. You have recently cut your hair shorter; the difference in colour between the back of your neck and the rest of your exposed skin is testament to that. I also deduce you are in mourning, as you still wear black cufflinks, which suggest it is a relative or a close friend who has died. Finally, I don't need Dr Watson's astute medical knowledge to tell me that you have been in considerable distress. It is clear from your short ragged nails and from the dark rings under your eyes. Pray tell me the facts so I can evaluate them."

Brett's blue eyes danced in silent amusement for a moment, marveling at the cleverness of this detective, then became dulled again as he remembered the seriousness of his situation. Brett closed his eyes and sighed. The heavy burden he had been carrying for the past year *was* overwhelming and it would be a relief to share at least part of it with someone. He had heard of Sherlock Holmes from the stories in *The Strand Magazine*. In fact, both he and Danny had decided to seek his help yesterday, *how ironic it is to find myself here. But how much should I tell him?* mused Brett. He could not, would not endanger the lives of these two gentlemen. Brett resolved to reveal as much as he dared. Suddenly, he noticed the drawing of the waterfall hanging over the mantelpiece and felt a shiver go down his spine. He cleared his throat and inhaled deeply.

"Mr Holmes, Dr Watson, before I begin, I must let Danny know where I am. He travelled down to London with me and we were staying at the Richmond Hotel; would it be possible for me to get word to him?"

"Mrs Hudson!" cried Holmes, startling both Brett and Watson.
The door to the living room opened and Mrs Hudson appeared, now recovered from her shock of earlier.

"Ah, Mrs Hudson," said Holmes. "Would you be so kind as to send a wire to the Richmond Hotel on behalf of Mr Sullivan here, addressed to Mr Danny..."

"Peterson," said Brett, responding to Holmes's questioning glance.

"Mr Danny Peterson," continued Holmes, "to inform him that his friend is safe here in Baker Street."

Mrs Hudson nodded and turned to leave.

"Thank you, Mrs Hudson," said Holmes after her.

Brett thanked Holmes. *I hope Danny is all right,* thought Brett; a feeling of dread had come over him for Danny's safety.
Well, there's nothing I can do for him at present. Watson passed Brett a glass of water. Brett unsteadily raised the glass and gulped down the water. It was time to begin talking, time for the unspoken truths to be heard.

Chapter Five

Brett began by recounting the events which took place a year ago, culminating with Matthew's death at Lodore Falls.

"Mr Holmes, it was not until I received the watch that I realised my cousin had been murdered. I knew Matthew would never have parted with his pocket watch unless it was for a very good reason. I examined the watch, thinking that perhaps it was broken, but when I opened the back, I found a small piece of paper hidden inside."

Holmes leaned forward, intrigued by what Brett had said so far, and looked at Watson who was also listening intently and taking notes in his ever-present notebook. Holmes motioned Brett to continue.

"Well, Mr Holmes," said Brett, "when I unfolded the piece of paper, I saw that the formula for a new type of explosive was written on it. My cousin had also written an additional message to me, which simply said, 'forgive me for the pain I will cause'. That, I believe, was further indication that something was terribly amiss with his death at the Falls."

Holmes nodded and asked, "The formula, do you still have it?"

Brett smiled grimly. "If you mean the original piece of paper, yes, I do, but it is secured in a personal vault at

Barnetts, Hoares, Hanbury, and Lloyd in Lombard Street.[2] It was the safest place I could think of, given that this formula has cost blood already. However, if you want to know what the formula is, I have memorized it."

"If you would be so kind, Mr Sullivan. I have some knowledge of chemistry and this formula would be of interest to me," remarked Holmes. "Watson, can you get some paper and a pencil?"

Watson put down his notebook, went over to the desk bureau, retrieved the pencil and paper, and gave them to Brett, who wrote down the formula. Brett handed the paper to Watson, who, in turn, passed it to Holmes. Holmes's eyes widened when he read the formula and he looked up at Brett.

"This formula is for gelata lignis, which, translated from Latin would be known as Gelignite explosive, a revolutionary development in the field of explosives. [3] Were you aware of what this formula was for, Mr Sullivan?" asked Holmes.

Astonished by Holmes's analysis of the formula, Brett looked at Watson. Watson smiled and said proudly to Brett, "Holmes has a formidable knowledge of chemistry."

---

[2] This bank did exist and eventually grew to become Lloyds TSB Bank, one of the Big Four banks in the UK.
[3] The earliest known form of plastic explosive, invented by Alfred Nobel in 1875.

Addressing both of them, Brett answered Holmes's question, "I did know what the formula was for but I don't understand the chemistry or how it is made. All I knew was that a friend gave it to Matthew to experiment with to see if it really would make blasting rock easier, as part of the company's civil engineering project. He had already tried it in a limited capacity and the results were promising. That's why he wanted financial backing to expand the experiment and produce larger amounts of the substance."

"And I am willing to wager it was not long after this that your cousin started to receive the threats," said Holmes.

Brett took another gulp of water and sighed.

"That's right. After Matthew's funeral, Danny and I went back to the office to sort out the paperwork and we discovered the threatening letters."

Appalled by what he was hearing, Watson looked up from his notebook.

"Did you report this to the police, to that Inspector Roche who was conducting the investigation into your cousin's death?"

"Yes, I did," said Brett, his blue eyes darkening with anger at the memory. "He dismissed the evidence and said it was not directly linked to Matt's death at the Falls. Danny and I were infuriated at the coroner's inquest when the evidence was not produced and even though Danny and I protested in the most vigorous terms, the coroner still gave a verdict of accidental death. Accidental death my foot, it was murder, Mr Holmes, I tell you!"

Brett was shaking with rage and the sudden movement jarred his ribs, causing him to cry out in pain. Watson was at Brett's side in an instant, fearing Brett had caused himself further injury.

"It's all right, Doctor," said Brett to reassure a concerned Watson. "I let my anger get the better of me."

"I believe you, Mr Sullivan, from the evidence you have told me so far. I am sorry you had to experience such a poor example of what British justice can do. I will endeavour to correct that, but you have more to tell us, otherwise you would not be sitting here in Baker Street recovering from your injuries. Please, continue your narration of events and give me the facts as they occurred," said Holmes, irritated by the emotional interruption to his train of thoughts.

Brett was hurt by Holmes's remarks but Holmes did have a point, he should not have let himself get so angry. Brett rubbed his eyes, trying to keep at bay the throbbing that threatened to cloud his own thoughts. Brett's obvious exhaustion caused Watson some concern, but before Watson could say anything, Brett began to speak once more.

"I'm sorry, Mr Holmes. This is rather difficult for me, but you are right; there is much more I have to tell you." Brett swallowed hard and continued.

"After the coroner's inquest, Danny and I decided to conduct an investigation of our own. We went through the threatening letters with a fine-toothed comb and examined the company records for details of the creditors Matthew had approached. Then we began to make enquiries. We learnt that most of the creditors with whom Matthew had corresponded were of good faith and had, in fact, declined to get involved with the funding of an unproven product. But there was one firm--Sykes Holdings, Ltd.--which expressed an interest and Matthew had accepted their financial assistance. As both Danny and I were to discover, that firm was a front for a far more sinister organisation which we came to know as the James Gang."

Raising his eyebrows at that, Holmes looked at Watson, leapt up from his chair, and began pacing the room, twirling to face Brett.

"That is indeed of considerable interest, as I have heard of this gang being active in several recent cases of mine. Please continue, Mr Sullivan."

"Before Danny came to serve in my regiment in South Africa, he had served a few months in the military police, so he was able to utilise his experience and knew the types of questions to ask. Of course, the more questions we asked and the deeper we got into our private investigation, the more attention we attracted; the James Gang did not take kindly to our activities."

Watson looked up and asked, "And that's when you both started receiving threatening letters?"

Holmes glanced at Watson, suppressing a chuckle. *Watson's deduction skills are improving by the day,* he thought with a surge of pride.

"Yes, that's right, Doctor," said Brett, continuing his narration.

"Three months ago, things started to take a turn for the worse when Danny was attacked on his way home from the company office, which had become a base of our investigation. He was beaten and his leg was broken in the attack. It was then that we realised that we were no longer safe and decided to go on the run like common criminals. We were constantly looking over our shoulders and, therefore, noticed that this James Gang had people following us every step of the way. Eventually, a fortnight ago, we arrived in London. We had hoped we would be safe here, and for a while, nothing happened. We began to breathe more easily, thinking that we had shaken off our pursuers. That is, until last night, when we received a direct threat to both of our lives. We found our hotel room ransacked, and then, during the night, an intruder broke into our room and tried to smother me. Fortunately, Danny is a light sleeper and my struggle to free myself from the attacker awakened him. He managed to fend the attacker off and received a stab wound to his arm for his efforts. That was the second time my sergeant has saved me from certain death."

Brett closed his eyes and slumped back against the couch, exhausted after his long speech. He accepted another glass of water. Determined to finish his tale, he resumed, "It was then that we decided we had to come to see you. So this morning I told Danny to stay at the hotel and went to enquire as to your address. On my way back to the hotel, I was attacked yet again. I was walking down a little side street, a shortcut I had come to know and use. The horse and carriage were being driven wildly and I was caught in their path. There was very little I could do to escape, except try to throw myself clear, and I barely did so in time, landing heavily on my shoulder. Before I had time to recover from this incident, I was hauled off the ground by a thoroughly unpleasant man. He said he had a message for me and proceeded to attack me, punching me in the chest and stomach, then throwing me to the ground once more. He said Mr James had run out of patience and the time for words was over."

Holmes sat back down in his chair, having stood at the mantelpiece listening to his client's narrative.

"Do you know who this James fellow is?" asked Holmes in a not-quite-steady voice, thereby immediately attracting Watson's attention and concern. *Why was Holmes becoming distressed?* thought Watson.

"No, Danny and I have never met him, but it is our understanding that he is the leader of this gang; after all, it is known as the James Gang."

Brett felt guilty because he had not told the whole truth on this particular point. He was certain of the gang leader's identity but could not prove it. If he was right, then Sherlock Holmes and Dr Watson were in mortal danger, and he would not allow them to be hurt. *The James Gang can do what they like to me, but I'll not have more blood on my hands,* thought Brett who once again became concerned about his sergeant and friend Danny Peterson.

It was Watson who broke the short silence, noticing the lines of fatigue clearly etched on Brett's face and wanting to bring the interview to a close so that his patient could rest.

"Can you remember anything more after your assault this morning?" he asked.

Brett closed his eyes. His head was pounding now and he knew he could not stay awake for much longer.

"No, Doctor, I don't remember much. Just flashes, I must have been disoriented after the attack. I suppose in my confusion I was drawn here because Danny and I had decided earlier on to consult you, Mr Holmes."

Holmes nodded.

"Thank you, Mr Sullivan, for telling me all the facts. Your case is most intriguing, but you must rest now and I have much to consider."
Brett felt his eyes become heavier. Although it was now well into morning, Brett was exhausted by lack of sleep

and pain from his injuries. Watson saw the flicker of pain play across Brett's face and prepared a dose of morphine, but his patient caught Watson's arm, stopping him. Brett had to ask Holmes one more question.

"Mr Holmes, I have told you the facts as I know them, but what I want to know is why? Why is this gang so desperate to obtain the formula?"

Holmes looked straight into Brett's eyes, almost boring holes into him.

"That is the heart of the matter, Mr Sullivan, why indeed."
Brett felt a sharp prick as Watson injected him with morphine. As Brett succumbed to sleep, his thoughts turned to Danny. *Oh Danny, be safe, my friend.*

Watson gently covered Brett with a blanket and looked at Holmes, who was now staring out of the window. Watson felt a sense of foreboding and tried to fight the fear that was building within him. The same fear he had felt these past few nights. He sighed softly.

"Holmes, Mr Sullivan is asleep now, what do you make of this case?"

Holmes turned round to face Watson, seeing the fear clearly showing on Watson's face.

"My dear Watson, I suspect that Mr Sullivan and his friend are in grave danger and that this case is far deeper and more dangerous than we have encountered for some time. I would advise you to remain armed at all times until this is over."

Watson swallowed hard, "I will, Holmes, I promise."

Giving Watson a reassuring smile, Holmes returned his gaze to the street outside. The smog had built up particularly densely that morning, *like an evil stench smothering this city,* thought Holmes, *but not as evil as the fog of evil I sense in this case.* Holmes returned to his chair, lit a pipe, and closed his eyes. He began to contemplate what was said, what deductions could be drawn from the evidence he had heard, and what lay ahead.

Sitting in a chair next to the settee, Watson watched over his patient. He glanced at Holmes and back at Brett, and then stared at the flickering flames of the coal fire, dreading what may yet come. *Whatever happens,* thought Watson, *I'll stand with you, Holmes.*

In the street below, a lone figure leaned against a lamp post, looking up at the window of 221B. He was dressed in a long cloak which hid his face; only his eyes glinted malevolently from underneath the hood. He gave a snarl of contempt. Having observed Brett collapsing on the steps of the flat and being taken in, the stranger was angered even more. *They will pay,* he thought. As the cloaked stranger turned to walk away from Baker Street and disappear into the London smog, a chilling smile crossed his lips as he began to plan just how heavy a price that would be.

Chapter Six

Danny Peterson spent the last hour pacing up and down his hotel room. Brett had told him, *no, ordered,* thought Danny, to stay at the hotel and wait for his return. That had been two hours ago and there was still no sign of his friend and former commanding officer. No longer able to endure the wait, Danny put on his coat and was ready to go out, determined to find Brett. Just as he was about to leave the room, there was a knock on the door and Danny opened it to find the hotel messenger standing there.

"Message, sir, arrived this morning." The messenger handed Danny a piece of paper and walked away. Danny closed the door, walked to the writing desk, and sat down to read the message.

If you want information about the death of Matthew Crowther, meet me at The Spread Eagle & Crown[4] at Rotherhithe. I will await you there. You won't know me but I will recognise you.

Danny felt a surge of anger and fear growing within him. Every instinct he possessed told him this was a trap. He also knew that he did not have much of a choice because the James Gang knew that he and Brett

---

[4] This pub was established in the 1600s and known as the Shippe pub before being rebuilt in the 1620s and renamed the Spread Eagle and Crown.

were staying at the hotel, *last night's events had shown that all too painfully,* thought Danny as he rubbed his arm, still aching where he had been stabbed. Danny reasoned that, despite the danger, he might be able to glean some new information that could help Brett.

Danny began to write on a sheet of hotel stationery letter paper, the pencil shaking in his hand.

My dear Captain and friend,

    Please forgive me for breaking your orders for only the second time under your command. But I must pursue a new lead in our investigation. Everything tells me this is a trap and I fear that this adventure into the unknown may well be a dangerous one. Whatever happens, please know that I have always been your friend and that I couldn't have asked for a better commanding officer and companion in South Africa and afterwards. I want you to know how much I value our friendship. If I could have chosen someone to call 'brother', it would have been you. I shall always stand beside you, whether in life or in death.

Yours,

Danny.

Danny stared at the short letter he had just written. He knew how significant the letter was. He had faced the possibility of not coming back from a battle many times in South Africa. Danny knew that he was not going into battle this time, but he sensed the danger and the fear of not coming back was as real now as it was back then. Danny placed the letter into an envelope, marked it for the attention of Captain Brett Sullivan, and left the letter propped up against the inkbottle on the small writing table. He took one last look around the room, closed the door behind him, and walked out of the hotel into the hazy smog-filled morning. He called for a cab and gave the order to take him to Rotherhithe.

Rotherhithe Docks was a flurry of activity. Danny heard the seagulls squealing above him; they were dive-bombing the quayside in search of food, and the commotion they caused sent water splashing in all directions. All around him, Danny could see ships moored by the quayside, workers pushing wheelbarrows of cargo to the various warehouses scattered across the docks, and people going about their business. He shielded his eyes from the morning sun as the smog had dissipated with the fresh wind that blew in from the river. He had to find the pub in which he had been told to meet his contact.

After half an hour of searching, he found it, pushed the door open, and entered the smoke-filled room. The smell of tobacco assaulted Danny's nostrils. As he looked around, Danny could see no obvious sign of anyone waiting for him. *Might as well buy myself a drink,* mused Danny. Danny slapped down a few coins on the bar and a barmaid came up to him. She was blond, with her long hair touching her shoulders, the curls adding shape and bounce to her tresses. She was no more than thirty, but her hazel eyes told a story of their own. She had seen all of life walk through that door, and the Danny's slightly disheveled and worn look did not bother her in the least.

"'Ere what can I get you?" asked the barmaid, somewhat impatiently.

35

"A pint of Bass, please,"[5] said Danny, shifting nervously in his seat, his eyes darting around in search of someone who looked like he was waiting. His search was in vain, however, and Danny drank the beer that had been placed in front of him. *Maybe this had been a wild goose chase after all,* thought Danny. He was about to get up and leave, when suddenly something pushed against his side, causing him to give out an involuntary yelp.

"What the--"

"Shut up and do exactly as I say," said Danny's assailant.
Danny's eyes were as hard as steel as he stared at the unfriendly stranger. He knew he had to gain control of this potentially dangerous encounter.

"Who are you?"

"Follow me and I will tell you what you want to know."

Danny nodded and got up to follow this mysterious stranger out of the back entrance. This turn of events alarmed Danny but he had to see this through. Discreetly, he slipped his hand into his coat pocket and felt the welcome touch of cold gunmetal against his palm. Soon, Danny found himself on a shingle beach,

---

[5] The Bass & Co Brewery was established by William Bass in 1777 and was one of the first breweries in Burton upon Trent. It quickly expanded to become one of the most recognized English beer brands and was popular in Victorian England.

and saw the tidal waves of the Thames lapping up against the shoreline. The beach was perfectly secluded from the busy bustle of Rotherhithe Docks. Danny tightened his grip on the old service revolver. He did not like this in the least.

"All right, what information do you have for me, mister?" asked Danny.

The stocky but well-built man smiled malevolently, his smile displaying blackened teeth with a gold filling in one of the molars. Two more men joined him from the shadows; one of them wielded a nasty-looking club which he was softly but menacingly tapping against his palm.

"Hey, I thought you had information for me, not an invitation to a bar brawl!" Danny's attempt at humour hid the very real fear he felt.

"Wrong, Mister, your friend is dead and you are next. Mr James says if you give him the formula you just might get out of here alive, if you don't, well…"

Danny whipped out his revolver from his pocket and prepared to fire, but he was too late. He had not seen another figure come out of the shadows who struck him hard on his arm with a heavy metal bar. Danny fell to the ground, howling as streaks of red-hot pain shot up his arm and he clutched it trying to control the pain to no avail. Danny was grabbed off the ground and his face came close to that of his attacker, Danny felt the man's foul breath on his face.

"Are you going to tell us what we want to know?"

"Go to hell!"

Danny knew he was not going to get out of this alive.
But if my death saves the life of my captain, so be it,
thought Danny grimly.

Angered by his response, his attackers began to beat
him with the heavy metal bars and clubs. In the
seclusion of this jetty, Danny's screams could not be
heard by the outside world. As Danny cringed in pain
from the never-ending onslaught of blows, he felt
himself being dragged, and, suddenly, water covered his
face. Danny gasped for breath as the water began to fill
his lungs. He felt himself being lifted out of the water,
and as he greedily gulped at the air, he heard a voice, as
if from afar.

"Where is it? Where have you put the formula?"

Exhausted and in pain, Danny wished this never-ending
question would stop. "You can kill me, but you will
never find the formula. I'll see you in hell first!"

Danny was plunged into the watery depths again and
this time his whole body convulsed. Strong hands
wrapped tightly around his neck, compressing his
windpipe and he felt his eyes burn as he felt his life
drain from him. His sight was fading now but through
the water Danny saw figures hover above him, one face
stood out, white-haired and horribly disfigured. Danny

shut his eyes; he did want the last thing he saw to be that horrible vision. In one last desperate attempt to free himself, Danny lashed out wildly with his arms, but strong hands held his torso down and Danny saw the last few the precious air bubbles escape from him and rise to the surface. Danny felt his body involuntarily convulse until the convulsion became less and less violent, turning into merely a slight shudder. *I'm so sorry Brett, I failed you, please forgive me.* Danny's final thoughts gave way to the encroaching darkness; he could no longer see. To his surprise, Danny felt an overwhelming sense of peace, and then nothingness. Danny Peterson, late of the Victoria Column and holder of the British South Africa Company Medal, was dead.

Chapter Seven

The morning passed slowly at 221B Baker Street. The thud of coal ashes periodically dropping into the grate tray below was the only sound heard in the sitting room. It was Holmes who broke the silence at long last, standing up and stretching his lean frame:

"Watson, I am going to the Richmond Hotel to see if I can find more clues to help us in this investigation. It is also of concern to me that Mr Peterson has not replied to my telegram. I see your patient is still asleep, so please remain here. I will be back soon."

Watson looked at Holmes, clearly unhappy at the prospect of Holmes going out on his own. *Hadn't Holmes said this was a dangerous case and advised me to keep a revolver with me at all times?* thought Watson with some trepidation. Watson desperately wanted to remain at Holmes's side, but he knew he could not abandon his patient.

"Be careful, Holmes," said Watson, the images from his recent nightmares still prominent in his mind.

"I shall be, my dear fellow. I don't expect any trouble, but I have my revolver with me," replied Holmes, patting his jacket pocket.

Holmes gave Watson a shadow of a smile which was instantly replaced by his usual impassive expression.

He will be safe in Baker Street, thought Holmes, looking at Watson and Brett for the final time before opening the door to the landing and closing it behind him. Holmes walked down the stairs, meeting Mrs Hudson who was waiting by the front door to let him out.

"Mrs Hudson, I shan't be long, but please take care of them for me and don't let anyone in other than myself," instructed Holmes.

The long-suffering landlady smiled. She knew how much Holmes cared for Dr Watson (although he'd never admit to it), just as much as Dr Watson cared for Holmes. It had been a privilege to have been a small part of that friendship and she loved them both as a mother loves her children.

"Don't worry, Mr Holmes, I have a nice pot of tea and some biscuits on the way for the doctor, he looked as if he needed it when I saw him earlier."

Holmes smiled at how observant Mrs Hudson was to have noticed Watson's troubled sleep. He gently kissed her hand in a rare show of affection and then went out into the busy London Street to hail a cab that would take him to Richmond Hotel. Climbing into the cab, Holmes glanced up at his lodgings and hoped that he had made the right decision in leaving Watson alone. Holmes settled back in his seat, determined to put his concerns to the back of his mind, and used his stick to signal to the cabbie that he was ready. The hansom was soon making its way from Baker Street to the hotel and

Holmes was wrapped in thought about what lay ahead. Before long, the hansom arrived at the hotel. and Holmes got out of the cab, paid the driver, and walked into the hotel lobby. A surly receptionist, a young man of no more than twenty-five, greeted him.

"Can I get you anything, sir?" asked the receptionist. Holmes replied,

"Yes. My name is Sherlock Holmes. Can you tell me if the telegram I wired to this hotel earlier this morning was delivered to a Mr Danny Peterson?"

The receptionist walked over to his duty book, flicked through the pages, took a note out of a pigeon hole and walked back over to where Holmes was waiting impatiently, drumming his fingers on the desk.

"Well sir, it arrived, but when the messenger boy went up to deliver it, he found that Mr Peterson was gone, and has not been back since."

Holmes looked at the receptionist with disdain.

"And you did not even think to send a reply, to advise me of that?"

Holmes's mood suddenly darkened as he clenched his jaw in frustration.

"What room is Mr Peterson staying in?" asked Holmes curtly, in no mood for excuses.

The receptionist had turned pale and swallowed hard at seeing Holmes's expression. Obviously, this Sherlock Holmes was not a man to be trifled with. The receptionist decided the best course of action was to give Holmes the information he demanded.

"Room 1710, sir," replied the receptionist meekly.

Holmes wasted not another second at the receptionist's desk. Given the gravity of this case, he was worried about the safety of his client's friend. He darted up the stairway and walked briskly down the corridor leading to the room, his sharp eyes taking in the maid making the bed in a vacant room, quickly observing that she was struggling with her chores. *A new maid,* he thought, *she won't last the week here.* But Holmes's mind snapped back to the task in hand as he arrived at his destination.

The door is slightly ajar, observed Holmes, his senses now alert to the possibility of an intruder having broken into the room. Holmes lifted his cane and used it to open the door slowly but purposefully. A scene of chaos and destruction greeted him. Clothes were scattered everywhere, some thrown on the floor, other items half hanging out of dresser drawers, which had obviously been searched. The mattress had been shredded and feathers lay everywhere. Holmes carefully walked further into the room to assess the damage. Suddenly, a figure appeared from the bathroom, and for a moment, both the intruder and Holmes froze in surprise. The intruder, a well-built, stocky man with greying hair, recovered first and lunged forward at Holmes.

Holmes gripped his cane, using it to push back his attacker, who fell back, crashing into a chair. With a cold laugh, he got up and swung his fist at Holmes from the left, aiming at the jaw. Holmes ducked the first blow and delivered a punch of his own to his attacker's face, sending him sprawling to the floor. The intruder recovered quickly and grabbed a chair, raising it over Holmes and smashing it down on him. This time it was Holmes who fell to the floor face down. Holmes shook his head in a futile attempt to clear it and rose unsteadily to face his attacker once again.

Taking advantage of Holmes's groggy state, the intruder delivered a left hook into Holmes's face. As a result, Holmes staggered backwards, the back of his head slamming against the stone mantelpiece. Holmes felt his legs buckle and fell to the floor with a thud, face upwards. His vision blurred, stars danced before his eyes, and the room began to spin. Holmes struggled to push himself back up but his effort only brought white hot spikes of pain piercing his skull, overwhelming him until Holmes's world blacked out. A trickle of blood slowly formed next to Holmes's head.

The intruder stood back, at first pleased with his handiwork, then panicking when he saw the blood. Not knowing if his attack had left Holmes alive or dead, the intruder turned and fled the scene, leaving Holmes alone and defenseless.

Chapter Eight

The afternoon sunshine inched its way across the silent room, spreading its golden fingers further and further and eventually settling on the still form that was sprawled on the floor. After a while, a moan escaped from the man's lips and he stirred slightly. Slowly and painfully, Holmes opened his eyes and immediately shut them again tightly as the bright light sent waves of pain through him. He struggled to get up, groping his way round, using the mantelpiece, once a source of his downfall, now an invaluable aid. Slowly, Holmes stood upright, leaning heavily against the stone mantelpiece. He rubbed his forehead, wishing the room would stop spinning. Holmes cast his weary eyes around the room until they settled on the writing desk, which had remained undisturbed by the thief. Holmes must have interrupted him before he had a chance to rifle through the desk's contents. Holmes staggered across the room, almost crashing into the dressing table, and was grateful for the one chair that remained undamaged after the fight. He sat down heavily, cursing his throbbing head, and glanced at the surface of the desk. His eyes fixed upon the envelope propped up against the ink bottle. The envelope was addressed to Captain Brett Sullivan-- his client. Picking up the envelope, Holmes deposited it in his coat pocket. There was nothing else of interest to be found. Holmes took out his pocket watch and was unpleasantly surprised to discover how long he had lain unconscious. *Almost two hours*, Holmes thought, and then became worried as he knew Watson would be distressed by his prolonged absence. Holmes heard a gasp of surprise and looked up to see the maid standing in the doorway, eyes wide in shock and fear. Holmes raised his hand in an attempt to reassure her that he meant no harm to her, but the maid ran off, terrified.

Slowly and unsteadily, Holmes stood up and immediately regretted it as the room began to spin round once again. He lurched forward and unsteadily walked across the room. This effort had exhausted Holmes, and he had to lean against the door frame to catch his breath. Slowly, he made his way down the corridor and down the stairs, almost stumbling at one point. Hotel guests stopped in their stride as they watched the tall lean man unsteadily make his way to the hotel entrance and outside to the line of cabs. Holmes by now was looking pale and drawn and leant heavily on his cane, his head pounding with each step he made. Holmes tried to call for a cab, but trying to speak caused another spike of numbing pain to go through his head and Holmes leant heavily against a lamppost, trying to control the pain.

"Sir, you look you like you could use a ride to the hospital," said a gruff but kindly voice.

Holmes looked up and saw a cabbie perched on top of his hansom, looking down at him with concern.

Holmes smiled and replied hoarsely, "Take me to 221B Baker Street."

The cabbie nodded in acknowledgement and Holmes stumbled into the hansom. He closed the door, sank back into his seat, and closed his eyes with a soft moan.

All Holmes could think of was getting home and seeing Watson once more.

The screaming in Baker Street was reaching a crescendo and Dr Watson was struggling to wake his sleeping patient who was lashing out in the midst of a violent nightmare. "Mr Sullivan, wake up, man!" cried Watson, shaking his patient by both shoulders. It was not working.

"*Wake up!*" cried Watson once more.

Suddenly, Brett grabbed Watson by the throat, his hand tightening around it. Watson began to choke and tried to pull free from the surprisingly strong grip.

"Mr Sullivan... Brett... you are choking me... stop..." rasped Watson.

Brett suddenly bolted upright with a cry and then his eyes flicked open; he looked round the room, disoriented.

"What...where..." started Brett, confused.

Brett then saw, to his embarrassment, that his hands were still around Watson's throat. He withdrew his hands in horror and sank back down, covering his face with both hands as he realised what had happened.

"Forgive me, Doctor," said Brett, clearly upset both by the nightmare and by his own behavior.

47

Watson gulped in some air, undoing his collar and rubbing his neck.

"It wasn't your fault, Mr Sullivan; you were not responsible for your actions."

Brett opened his eyes and stood up, wincing as the movement hurt his ribs. He noticed, however, that the throbbing in his head has now subsided to a dull ache; he looked at Watson and smiled weakly, grateful for the doctor's understanding. He owed Watson an explanation.

"Doctor, I'm sorry, it's just that I have bad nightmares, South Africa left its mark on me, you see."

Watson smiled sympathetically, placing a gentle hand on Brett's shoulder.
"I understand, I was in Afghanistan myself and I saw things there that I would rather not remember as well. Perhaps it would help if you talked about it," said Watson, suddenly thinking how ironic it was that Holmes had said the very same thing to him that morning.

Brett considered Watson's words. It would be good to speak to someone other than Danny about his time in South Africa and he did owe Watson that after nearly choking him a few moments earlier. So Brett and Watson talked of the time they served in Her Majesty's Army, sharing their experiences. It was almost two hours later that Watson stood up and looked at his pocket watch. *Holmes has been gone far too long,* he thought, beginning to worry. *Where is he?* Watson walked over to the window and looked out.

The jolt of the hansom cab which was pulling up to stop at its final destination awakened Holmes, who had drifted off during the journey. His head was still pounding and Holmes wished it would stop. Disoriented, Holmes looked out of the window and realised he was in Baker Street. *Home,* thought Holmes.

Holmes stumbled out of the cab, almost falling onto the pavement. He leant heavily against the cab as he dug into his pocket to pay for the journey.

"On the house, sir," said the cabbie, smiling kindly at his passenger. The ageing cabbie never normally gave a free ride but he had recognised that the man needed help, and he would not charge a ride for a clearly unwell passenger.

Holmes looked up in surprise and his grey eyes softened. It was not often he found such kindness, since his own profession dealt with the darker side of humanity.

"Thank you, I am most grateful," replied Holmes.

Holmes turned round and looked at his front door. It seemed such a long way off, but he was determined to walk the short distance. Leaning heavily on his cane, Holmes walked stiffly and slowly to the front door. His legs almost gave way as he reached the railings. Holmes clung onto them for support, resting his head on his arms for a moment, before he staggered up the steps to his front door.

Watson had been worriedly looking out of the window for the last five minutes. *Maybe I should get a cab to the hotel,* he thought and then remembered that he had a patient to look after.
Watson rested his head against the window and closed his eyes for a moment, battling against the rising unease. The sound of a cab pulling up outside his lodgings made him look up.

A man stumbled out of the cab and only then he realised with dismay that it was Sherlock Holmes. Watson's chest tightened as the memories of his nightmares came flooding back. He rushed down the stairs, flung open the front door, and caught the stumbling detective just in time.

"Holmes, talk to me, are you all right?" Watson's voice was as unsteady as his hands, as he tightened his grip on Holmes.
Seeing the doctor's distress, Holmes hastened to reassure his friend.

"I'm all right, old man, just a bump on the head," Holmes gripped Watson's arm and smiled weakly.

"You're not all right, Holmes. You're hurt."

Watson placed Holmes's arm around his own shoulders and with his arm round Holmes' waist, helped his friend up the seventeen steps into their sitting room.

Brett, hearing the commotion, had lifted himself off the couch and was leaving heavily against the dining table. On entering the sitting room, Watson saw the empty couch and shot Brett a look of thanks as he settled Holmes down. Reaching for his medical bag, he immediately examined the head wound and saw that Holmes had more than just a bump on his head; rather, it was a deep cut that needed stitches. Watson injected Holmes with a sedative, to which Holmes did not object. The very fact that Holmes did not put up any resistance to his treatment indicated to Watson just how hurt Holmes had been.

"What happened, Holmes?" said Watson quietly, his voice still not quite steady, as he prepared the suture materials.

"I was investigating Mr Sullivan's hotel room when I was attacked by an intruder. Mr Sullivan, I found this letter addressed to you," said Holmes, who groped inside his pocket for the envelope and on finding it, placed the letter on the seat next to him. Holmes continued, his voice becoming weaker from exhaustion.

"I deduce that the letter is from your friend Danny, Mr Sullivan. I did not see him at the hotel. I do have to caution you that, given my experience, he may be in danger."
Watson had finished stitching Holmes's wound and passed the letter to Brett. Watson watched as Holmes sank back on the couch wearily, and he himself sat down rubbing his own eyes, the adrenalin draining from

him and relief taking over as he knew Holmes would be all right. *Still, I should have been with him,* thought Watson with a twinge of guilt.

Brett had sat down, unable to remain standing any longer, and opened the envelope. He read the contents and stared blankly at the letter, refusing to acknowledge what had been written. Tears blurring his vision, he kept re-reading the two lines that had affected him the most:

If I could have chosen someone to call 'brother', it would have been you. I shall always stand beside you, whether in life or in death.

"No, no, Danny, no!" cried Brett, crumpling up the letter. With a despairing look, he bowed his head. Watson got up from his chair and walked over to Brett, gently removed the crushed letter from Brett's hand and read the contents, then passed it to Holmes.

"It is as I feared, Mr Sullivan, we must go and look for your friend," said Holmes, who was looking pale and drawn, as he attempted to lever himself up. Strong hands held him back.

"Holmes, you are not going anywhere in your condition; it is almost evening now, and you need to rest until morning at least," remonstrated Watson.

Holmes was about to argue when the door to the sitting room opened and Mrs Hudson walked in with the evening paper.

Watson took the paper from Mrs Hudson and placed it on the dining table, walking back over to Holmes. He had no intention of letting Holmes out tonight.

Brett looked at them both and smiled briefly as they reminded him of his friendship with Danny; he would have protected Danny exactly as Watson was now protecting Holmes. Not wanting to intrude, Brett picked up the paper and his blood ran cold as he read the headline:

Body of War Veteran Found in Rotherhithe.

Brett's hands started trembling as he held the paper, his whole body went numb and he began to gasp for air as his chest tightened. Brett tried to get up, gasping once more for air, struggling to undo his collar.

Watson saw what was happening and rushed over to Brett.

"Take deep breaths, in through your nose, out through your mouth, in and out, slow and steady, that's it," said Watson as he loosened Brett's collar. Complying with Watson's instructions, Brett began to get his breathing under control.

Watson picked up the paper and silently passed it to Holmes.
After a few moments Brett stood up, clutching his side as his ribs protested. His hands were clenched tightly, his face darkened, and there was a steel glint in his eyes.

He stared straight at both Holmes and Watson as he spoke:

"You were right, Mr Holmes. Danny was indeed in danger and now he is dead. I will not rest until the person behind all this is brought to justice. I will catch this monster; I swear it as God is my witness."

Brett stared at the drawing of the Reichenbach Falls that hung over the mantelpiece.

I no longer fear the evil that had thrust its sharp jagged claws into my life for so long. I will get to the very heart of the James Gang and I will rip that heart out and tear it to shreds. Oh Danny, my dear friend, I am so sorry I failed you, but I swear, I will unleash hell on the person behind this. So help me God.

Chapter Nine

Holmes awoke to the early morning sunshine and muffled voices. His head was still pounding and he groaned, wishing it would stop. *How did I get here?* wondered Holmes as he realised he was in his own bed. And then he remembered. Brett Sullivan had collapsed shortly after reading the newspaper; the shock had been too much for him. Watson had rushed over to assist him and lifted Brett to a nearby chair. Holmes had tried to get up to help Watson and had only succeeded in making Watson's job more difficult as he too had fallen back as the movement had sent his head spinning. He remembered only flashes after that, he had heard Watson cry out his name and felt strong hands support him and then a sharp stab of pain in his arm and very little else after that. *Watson must have carried me to my room and sedated me,* thought Holmes. Turning his head, he saw the rumpled cushion on chair next to his bed and realised Watson must have been up with him most of the night. The muffled voices were growing louder, and he was thus able to distinguish Watson's angry voice. He had to find out what the commotion was about and to help his friend. Holmes pushed back the covers and placed his hand on his nightstand for support as he slowly rose from his bed. At first, he felt very weak and his legs almost gave way again, but then Holmes steadied himself. As soon as the room stopped spinning, he moved forward to the partially opened door and listened to the argument taking place in the sitting room.

"Inspector Lestrade, Holmes is not well. He has a severe concussion and I am absolutely forbidding anyone to see him right now, let alone asking him to examine a body down by the docks. He is simply not up to it," said Watson, glaring at the inspector.

"But Doctor, I must insist..." Lestrade resumed and was interrupted by Watson once more.

"No, Inspector. I won't hear another word, Holmes is in my care and as a doctor I will not permit this outing."

Holmes moved forward, already having heard enough. Watson was trying to protect him, *my loyal friend*. Holmes recognised the fear in Watson's words and saw the dark rings under Watson's eyes. He had to put a stop to this.

"Inspector Lestrade, how nice to see you," said Holmes, extending his hand.

"Mr Holmes! Dr Watson told me that you had been attacked and were thus unavailable. I need you to come with me this morning to Rotherhithe to examine a body..."
Holmes put up his hand, halting Lestrade in mid-sentence.

"Yes, Lestrade, I am aware of it, it was in the papers last night. I will come and investigate as it pertains to the one case I have at the moment," Holmes replied, looking at a very pale Brett Sullivan and at a very angry

Doctor Watson. Watson had moved to Holmes's side, motioning Holmes to sit down.

"Holmes, I absolutely forbid you to go. You have had a serious head injury and I can't allow you to go out until you are fully recovered!" cried Watson.

Brett Sullivan was awake and listening from the couch where Watson had again placed him the previous night. His head was much clearer now, and he felt more alert, although his injured ribs still ached. Brett got up, trying to mask his pain. He had to put a stop to this quarrel. He knew the body the Inspector wanted Sherlock Holmes to see was Danny Peterson's. He was not about to let Danny's death be the cause of a fight between these people. Brett looked at all three men and said,

"Gentlemen, please, I must insist you stop arguing amongst yourselves. Danny was my friend and I want to see him." Brett almost choked on the final words with grief.

Holmes, Watson, and Lestrade all turned to face Brett and were for a moment silenced by his words. It was Watson who broke the silence.

"Mr Sullivan, I know this must be difficult for you, but you are in no fit state to be out and about yourself."

Holmes also cut in, "I agree with Watson, Mr Sullivan. You must remain at Baker Street."

Lestrade, who by now had clearly despaired that anyone at all would come, said nothing.

Brett continued, "I have made my decision and I will not give way on that. I shall go with Inspector Lestrade to Rotherhithe and see what those fiends have done to Danny."
Holmes and Watson looked at each other and then back at Brett.

"Very well, Mr Sullivan, then I insist on accompanying you, it will not do to let you go out unprotected," said Holmes. He walked slowly back to his room and shortly reappeared, wearing his coat.

"Are you coming, Watson?" asked Holmes, buttoning his coat and pulling on his gloves.

Too tired to argue with Holmes and Lestrade, Watson reached for his own coat and walking stick. Opening his desk drawer, he picked up his service revolver and placed it in his inner coat pocket. He hoped he would not have to use it but he felt much safer having it close to hand. He turned to face Holmes.

"Of course I'm coming, Holmes," replied Watson softly.

Smiling, Holmes took Watson's arm and called for Mrs Hudson to hail a cab. The small party went down the stairs together and climbed into the waiting cab. Holmes instructed the cabbie to take them to Rotherhithe. With a jerk, the cab set off, the horse's hooves picking up a steady pace. In the cab, each man was alone with his private thoughts and no one spoke until they arrived at Rotherhithe.

Two policemen standing outside the Spread Eagle and Crown Pub was the only indication that anything was amiss as Holmes, Watson, Brett, and Lestrade arrived at the scene of the crime. Lestrade led the way, taking them through to the back of the pub and out through the rear entrance which led to the beach below. The sea breeze whipped up and Brett shivered, wrapping his coat tightly round him. In the distance he could see the body lying on the beach. Brett shivered again, this time not from the cold but from fear. He felt a hand on his shoulder and turned to see Dr Watson, who said quietly,

"Are you sure you want to do this, Mr Sullivan? There is no shame in going back—on the contrary, it would be quite understandable."

His face a mask of resolve, Brett shook his head. He was going to see this through. He pushed past Holmes and Lestrade who had been talking and rushed to the body, falling to his knees as he reached it. The body was lying face down; Brett gently rolled it over and stared at Danny Peterson's face. It was battered and bruised, eyes staring endlessly into nothingness. Brett pulled up the body into his arms, cradling it from the wind, and began to rock gently, tears running down his face as buried his head against Danny's still form. Holmes and Watson watched as Brett cradled his dead friend. Lestrade started to move forward to stop Brett but Holmes held Lestrade back with a firm grip on his shoulder and said,

"No, Lestrade, leave him for a moment, he needs time to himself."

Although he was furious that the murder scene had been disturbed, Lestrade unhappily consented. Brett finally raised his head again and looked at Danny. He slowly laid Danny down and closed his friend's eyes. Picking up Danny's left hand, Brett gently slid the service ring off Danny's middle finger and placed it on his own. Putting his hand on Danny's head, Brett closed his eyes.

Why didn't you listen to me, my dear brave friend? You should not have gone out alone.

Brett squeezed his friend's left hand once more and gently laid it back down. He felt a hand on his shoulder and turned round to find Holmes and Watson standing behind him. Brett started to get up and let out a gasp; his ribs ached after he had been kneeling down for so long. Both Holmes and Watson gave Brett a hand up and he murmured his thanks. Suddenly, Brett turned even paler and rushed off down to the river. Clutching his side, he leant on a wooden beam and immediately began to be violently sick. Brett cried out and then clung on the wooden beam staring out at the Thames, watching the small tug boats go by, guiding the larger cargo boats down the Thames and out to sea.

Holmes caught Watson's arm, stopping him from going after Brett.

"No, Watson, give him some time to himself. He needs to be alone and does not desire company; otherwise he would have indicated it to us already."

Holmes bent down to the body and methodically began to examine the scene before him. He started by inspecting the fibres clinging to Danny's coat. Holmes reached inside his own coat pocket and pulled out a pair of tweezers and his magnifying glass. With the tweezers, Holmes carefully picked up the strand of fibre that had interested him.

Ah, thought Holmes, *this is a fibre from a working man's jacket, made of coarse brown cloth. The attacker had been wearing the jacket this fibre came from.* Next, Holmes lifted the dead man's hands and inspected them, again with his glass. He saw that Danny must have fired his gun—gunpowder residue was left on the back of his right hand. However, Holmes saw no gun anywhere near the body.

Next, Holmes examined Danny's coat pockets, pulling out the note instructing Danny to come to the Rotherhithe. *The note had been written by a learned man, not by one the rough heavies hired to kill Mr Peterson,* thought Holmes as he placed the note in his own pocket. There would be time to examine it in more detail later. Holmes moved away from the body lay prone on the ground, his outstretched hands gliding over the pebbles and sand. He could discern where indentations had been made by footprints and Holmes followed the trail down to the beach. He saw something catching the sun in the water, rolled up his sleeve, and put his hand in. He carefully scooped up the object and, to his surprise, discovered it was a medal. It must have fallen out of Danny's pocket during the struggle.

Watson, who had followed Holmes down to the beach, exclaimed,

"Holmes, that's the British South Africa Company Medal!"

Holmes nodded in acknowledgment. He turned the medal over and read the inscription on the back:

Awarded for gallantry shown on the battlefield in saving the life of Commanding Officer, Captain Danny Sullivan.

Holmes stood up and swayed, almost losing his balance.

"Holmes!" cried Watson, steadying him.

"It's all right, Watson, I just stood up too quickly."
Not convinced, Watson decided that this excursion had gone on too long. Holmes needed to rest.

"Inspector Lestrade, please go back to the cab with Holmes, I will be along shortly," instructed Watson, taking charge of the situation.

Lestrade offered no resistance; he was now feeling guilty about asking Holmes to come, seeing how pale he looked. Nodding in agreement, he said, "Come on, Mr

Holmes, you can tell me of your findings on our way back to the hansom."

Holmes looked at Watson and then at Danny. He placed the medal in Watson's hand. Instructions were not necessary. He knew that Watson would take good care of Danny.

"Don't be too long, Watson," said Holmes, as he turned and headed back to the hansom, his mind already beginning to analyse the clues he had found.

Watson watched as Holmes walked back with Lestrade, and then turned to see Brett down at the beach, slumped against the wooden beam. The wind was picking up and the cold was now biting; Watson rubbed his troublesome leg, which began to twinge once more as he made his way down to the beach. He approached Brett, who was staring blankly at the Thames.

"Mr Sullivan, please come back with us, there is nothing more to be gained by staying here. Holmes is waiting for us in the hansom."

Brett was clenching his hands into fists and then opening them again. He had hardly registered Watson's approach until he started speaking. His blue eyes dulled with pain and grief, Brett slowly turned to face Watson.

"Doctor, I failed him, I should have never left him. He saved my life and I lost his."

Watson placed his hand on Brett's shoulder and said gently,

"It wasn't your fault. You could not possibly have known what would happen and you must not blame yourself. Please come back with us--it is getting cold out here."

With a sad smile, Brett replied, "I'm all alone now, I've no friends or family left." Fingering Danny's service ring on his finger, Brett fought back tears.

"No!" said Watson. "You are not alone; Holmes and I will see this through to the end, find out who did this and bring justice."
Watson paused and handed Brett the medal Holmes had found in the water.

"He would have wanted you to have this. Don't you see? You will never be alone."

Brett felt the cold medal in the palm of his hand, stared at it and then held it tightly before placing it in his coat pocket. He could not allow himself to give up now, *for Danny's and Matthew's sakes,* thought Brett. The wind was indeed picking up and Brett turned up his coat collar, breathing deeply. He knew it was time to go back with Dr Watson. He stumbled forward; Watson took his elbow and, together, they walked back up to the waiting hansom. They paused briefly as Brett stopped at his friend's body one more time. It had been covered up and was being lifted onto a stretcher to be transported to the police morgue. Brett gently placed his hand on the body once more. *I will find the people who did this to you, my friend, I promise.*

Brett and Watson made their way back to the waiting hansom and Holmes watched as they both arrived, noting with concern that Watson was limping. Lestrade had gone back to Scotland Yard with the body and Holmes waited for Watson to arrive with Brett.

Once in all three of them were in the cab, Holmes signaled the driver to move off and sank back wearily into his seat. He required time to think about the case. Although he knew the cause and motives for this case, something was missing. Holmes had to know why they wanted the formula so badly. He needed to grasp that elusive missing link; above all, he had to protect both Watson and his client from the clutches of the James Gang. It was going to get more dangerous from this moment forward. Holmes closed his eyes and began to formulate some theories as to what that elusive missing link might be.

As the hansom disappeared into the busy streets, a heavily cloaked man watched it speed away; he had been watching everything through the window of a room in the abandoned house next to the Spread Eagle and Crown Pub from the moment Holmes had arrived. The man brushed back his straggly white hair.

So it is true then. Holmes is alive, looking very well for a previously dead man. It is a pity that he stands in my way, time is running out and I will have that formula. I don't care who tries to step in my way, all of them will be crushed.

The elderly man rose and left his vantage point, determined to carry out his plans. His James Gang would make sure of that. A chilling laugh echoed around the room as he left and closed the door behind him.

Chapter Ten

Mrs Hudson greeted her weary tenants and her guest as they returned to Baker Street. She frowned at them wishing they would rest. Perhaps the lunch she had prepared would help.
"Gentlemen, I have a cold lunch waiting for you upstairs, all of you look as if you could use some."

Holmes thanked Mrs Hudson and followed Watson and Brett up the stairs to the sitting room. He had no intention of eating right now; he needed to think. Holmes went over to his desk, opened the drawer, and saw his Moroccan case. *It would be tempting to just sit back and use it to get rid of this persistent headache,* mused Holmes as he ran his fingers over the case. *No! I need to think clearly and I must be alert for any sign of danger.* Holmes slammed the drawer shut, took up his pipe, stuffed it with tobacco from his Persian slipper, sat down in his favourite chair, and began to ponder the problem he had been asked to solve.

Watson looked at Brett who was sitting by the fire, his shoulders hunched up, staring into nothingness. He was still shaken by this morning's visit to Rotherhithe. *Who could blame him?* thought Watson. Brett has just lost his best friend, and Watson's mind flashed back to when he had thought Holmes was lying dead at the Reichenbach Falls. It had cut like a knife then and remembering his recent nightmares, Watson knew it still did. *I don't want to lose Holmes again,* thought Watson, as he sat down at the dinner table and looked at what was in front of him. He too was in no mood to eat, but he had to at some point *and so did they,* thought Watson glumly. He placed a sandwich on each of the three plates, placed one plate next to Holmes and another next to Brett, and then sat back at the table and proceeded to eat his own sandwich. Having finished, Watson moved to a chair by the fire, picked up *The Times,* and glanced over at Holmes and Brett. He noticed that Holmes had eaten his sandwich, but Brett had not.

Brett finally stirred and got up to leave. He felt he was imposing on Holmes and Watson; he was able to get around now despite the pain in his ribs and decided he should head back to the Richmond Hotel.

Hearing Brett get up to leave, Holmes opened his eyes and looked directly at Brett.

"Mr Sullivan, it is absolutely essential that you remain here. Going back to the Richmond Hotel is too dangerous and--"

Holmes stopped mid-sentence as he caught sight of an article on the front page of *The Times* Watson was reading. Holmes jumped up and grabbed *The Times* from Watson, much to his annoyance.

"*Holmes!* What the—..." said an exasperated Watson.

"I have been a blind fool!" exclaimed Holmes, reading the article quickly and then throwing the paper to the floor in annoyance.

Watson picked up the newspaper that had caused so much consternation and looked at the front page to see if he could find what had vexed Holmes so much. There was a report of fighting in South Africa, a high society marriage, an article about some very rare jewels from India that were currently in the vaults of the Bank of England for safekeeping whilst en route to an exhibition overseas, and the prospect of yet another increase in land duty taxes. Watson could not see anything that would have caused Holmes's reaction.

Holmes, ignoring the constant throbbing still troubling him from the knock to his head the night before, went to his bedroom and put on his coat. He smiled triumphantly as he came back out to greet the two startled men.

"Are you coming, Watson?" asked Holmes gleefully, his grey eyes shining expectantly.

"Coming? Coming where, Holmes?" asked Watson, realising that Holmes was on to something.

"The Bank of England, Watson, we have business to attend to there!"

Surprised, Watson glanced at Brett, who appeared equally surprised, then back at Holmes.

"The Bank of England, Holmes?"

"Yes, Watson, the Bank of England, to think I should have overlooked it!" said a frustrated Holmes.

"Mrs Hudson!" yelled Holmes, who was now on the landing.

Mrs Hudson appeared at the bottom of the stairway and looked up at Holmes.

"Ah, Mrs Hudson, would you be good enough to order a cab for us?"

The landlady walked outside and hailed a cab.

Holmes looked into the living room again and saw Watson helping Brett up and putting on his coat. He frowned. *Perhaps I should not have asked them to come with me*, he thought. *But I would be happier knowing that Watson is with me and not left on his own.*

Watson had seemingly read Holmes's mind, because he looked up at Holmes and smiled whilst helping Brett.

"We'll be all right Holmes, just give me a moment to get my own coat and I'll join you downstairs," said Watson.

Holmes went down the stairs with Brett, who held tightly onto the banister, beads of sweat running down the back of his neck. Joining Holmes outside the front door while waiting for the cab to arrive, Brett could contain his questions no longer.

"Mr Holmes, what has the Bank of England got to do with my cousin and Danny?" asked Brett, trying to hide his discomfort.

"It has everything to do with your case Mr Sullivan, I now know why the James Gang wants your formula so badly!" exclaimed Holmes triumphantly.

"However," continued Holmes, "I will explain everything soon enough, when Watson is here. Incidentally, where is Watson?" asked Holmes, looking up the stairs.

"Coming, Holmes!" cried Watson from the top of the stairs and walked down to join them.

Whilst talking with Brett, Holmes noticed a rough-looking man lurking by the newspaper stand opposite, sheltering in a bookshop doorway. The man was watching them intently. Holmes only cast a quick glance and acted as if he had not seen the watcher, glad of the convenient opportunity to observe whilst speaking to his client, but the fact that they were being watched outside their Baker Street flat sent a shudder down his spine. As they all climbed into the waiting hansom, Holmes knew that danger was never far away.

The journey to the Bank of England was not a long one and it was only a short while later that they arrived outside the front entrance of the bank. The surrounding street was a hive of activity. Well-dressed bankers were crossing the street going about their business, some of them laughing with their associates; the atmosphere was jovial, with a sense of opulence all around. Holmes, Watson, and Brett made their way to the foyer. A tall man, wearing a three-piece black suit with a fashionable tie-pin, the lines of long hours of study etched on his forehead, sat behind the main enquiry desk. He looked up condescendingly from behind the spectacles perched on the end of his nose at the party that had arrived at his desk.

"Yes, what can I do for you gentlemen?" he asked nonchalantly.

"My name is Sherlock Holmes and I wish to speak with the manager on a matter of some urgency," said Holmes.

"I beg your pardon?" said the receptionist, clearly irritated by the unexpected request.

Holmes was not in the mood for tittle-tattle. He read the receptionist's nameplate and responded,

"Mr Smythes, my time is limited and I cannot afford to waste it. I urge you again to inform the manager that I have urgent business to attend to with him regarding this bank."

The receptionist's face reddened and he said angrily,

"And I don't have time for you. If you want to see the manager you will need to make an appointment."

Holmes's face darkened; he was clearly irritated by Smythes's remark and was about to reply when he noticed a man walking into an office. Holmes recognised him instantly as being the manager and began to walk in his direction.

"Good morning, Mr Summers, might I have a moment of your time?" said Holmes loudly, his voice reverberating around the foyer.

Stepping in front of Holmes, the receptionist began to push him back.

"I warned you, Mr Summers is unavailable," he said.

Watson, who was standing next to Holmes, instinctively pushed himself in front of Holmes.

"Now look here, man, you are overstepping the mark, you will not push Holmes around again, do you hear?"

Holmes placed a restraining hand on Watson's shoulder and could feel the fine tremor. Realising Watson's nerves were decidedly shaky, Holmes said softly, "It's all right, Watson."
The commotion attracted the manager's attention. He stopped mid-stride and turned to face Holmes, recognising him instantly and walked over to him, appalled by the receptionist's behavior.

"Mr Holmes! It is such a pleasure to see you, especially after your invaluable aid in exposing the security flaws in the undiscovered underground sewage piping leading to the vaults. That certainly saved the Bank of England a great deal of embarrassment, not to mention monetary loss,"[6] said Summers, shaking Holmes's hand warmly.

Summers turned to the receptionist with contempt.

"Mr Smythes, I will not condone insolent behaviour to our customers, and particularly to Mr Sherlock Holmes. You are hereby dismissed from your post with immediate effect."
Summers turned back to Holmes, Watson, and Brett, smiling warmly.

"Pray, let us go to my office and tell me what your urgent business is, Mr Holmes," said Summers, gesturing in the direction of his office.

After all of them had settled down in the comfortable surroundings of the manager's office, Summers looked at Holmes expectantly.
"Well, Mr Holmes, perhaps now you would tell us the reason for your visit?"

Holmes leant forward in his chair.

---

[6] Such an incident did take place at the Bank of England (although well before Holmes's time, in 1836). The Directors of the Bank of England received an anonymous letter advising them of the existence of the sewer pipes that led directly to the vaults. The directors did not believe it until one night the vaults were successfully breached by a man climbing through the sewer pipes into the vaults.

"Mr Summers, I regret to inform you that the Bank of England is once again at risk for robbery. How secure are the Raji's imperial gold bullion bars that are currently stored in your vaults?"

There was a shocked silence in the room. Summers looked visibly shaken, and got up to pour himself a brandy from the decanter in the drinks cabinet situated behind him.

"Mr Holmes, how could you have possibly have known about the gold bullion? Only I and a select few knew about that, it is virtually a state secret."

Holmes chuckled. "I have my methods. You see, when I read in *The Times* of the Indian jewels placed in the vaults for safekeeping, it was simple for me to deduce that this coincided with a recent successful trade visit to India which my brother Mycroft was discussing with me at the Diogenes Club a few weeks ago."

Watson looked up from his notepad, raising an astonished eyebrow at Holmes's announcement, then smiling knowingly as he remembered the article in *The Times* that morning. His friend never ceased to amaze him.

"Mr Summers, it may have been a closely guarded secret but even the tightest of ships has rats in the cargo hold. In this case, some of these rats have connections with the James Gang who plan to steal the gold bullion which is currently in your bank's safekeeping."

Summers sat down heavily in his chair, trying to absorb what Holmes had just imparted to him.

"But Mr Holmes, no one can break into the vaults, they have the strongest doors of any bank in this country!"

Brett, who had been sitting quietly listening to the conversation, felt a growing sense of unease. He clenched his jaw; his anger was slowly beginning to build as he suddenly understood what had Holmes so agitated. *That blasted formula*, he thought, *which has caused the loss of the two people closest to me was wanted because someone planned to rob a bank?!* He could stand it no longer and blurted out with unguarded rage, "No, Mr Summers, they're not. Mr Holmes is trying to tell you that your precious vaults are in danger of having the bloody doors blown open by means of an explosive device not widely used before. I can't believe that men have died over this insane plot! If you'll excuse me, gentlemen, I need to get some air."

Brett stormed out of the room. Holmes, realising the danger Brett faced venturing out alone, quickly got up to go after him. Watson followed closely at his heels, leaving a shocked Summers slumped back in his chair.

Brett was almost outside the foyer when a man who had been waiting outside the entrance pounced on him, starting to lay in the punches thick and fast. One of the punches landed heavily on Brett's jaw and his injured ribs, causing him to cry out in pain.
Brett was sent reeling, falling to the floor. But he was so angry at learning what he just had that he got up quickly

and lunged forward at his attacker with a cry, landing a hard punch on his shoulder and continuing to hammer him down before kicking him hard in the stomach, which sent him crashing. But Brett's anger had not played out yet. Ignoring the pain in his ribs, Brett grabbed the attacker once more and pushed him hard against the wall.

"Why? For the love of God, tell me why?!"

The attacker laughed and Brett did not see the flash of a blade flicking open until after it was already plunged straight into his upper arm. Brett let out a cry of agony, releasing his attacker, and fell to the floor clutching his arm, trying to shut out the searing pain as the blood began seeping through his fingers. His attacker ran off into the busy London streets.

Holmes and Watson arrived on the scene just after that. Seeing the attacker had fled, Watson put the safety back on his revolver, thrust the revolver into his coat pocket, and bent down to aid Brett. Watson placed a clean handkerchief over the injured arm, secured it tightly, using his belt as a sling, and helped Brett up. Brett leant against the wall, breathing harshly, and said bitterly,

"I'm so sorry Mr Holmes, Dr Watson, I should not have lost control like that, I was just so enraged, all of this, Matthew, Danny, everything only for money's sake."

Holmes replied, "Your reaction is entirely understandable; in fact, it is I who owe you apologies for not telling you of my findings straight away. I am also sorry you were attacked. However, it does serve a very useful purpose in the long term because it will help bring this case to a successful conclusion."

Still supporting Brett, Watson looked up at Holmes and asked,

"How are we going to do that, Holmes?"

Holmes's eyes shone in anticipation.

"By setting a trap for the rats, my dear fellow. We will make them come to us and put an end to this case."

Brett and Watson looked at each other and back at Holmes.

"But...how, Holmes?" asked Watson, surprised.

"Elementary, my dear Watson, we shall give them the formula they'd been wanting and thus tighten the noose on the James Gang for once and all!"

Little did Holmes know how costly that noose would become.

Chapter Eleven

It had been two days since the visit to the Bank of England before the veiled advert in *The Times* was finally answered. Holmes had persuaded Brett to include a message in Danny's obituary. The message simply read that an item belonging to Mr James was available for collection at a safety deposit box at the Barnetts, Hoares, Hanbury, and Lloyd in Lombard Street. The item in question was a copy of the formula for the explosives. Holmes's plan had succeeded--Brett had received a telegram from the bank informing him of the removal of the formula from the deposit box.

Brett flexed his arm gingerly, thankful that he had not needed a sling because the knife injury was only superficial. He was worried by *The Times* advert and the possible response, feeling as if he had capitulated to the will of the James Gang.

"Mr Holmes, surely by giving them the formula you are inviting them to rob the bank? Also, won't they know it is a trap?" asked Brett with concern in his voice.

Holmes looked up and gave Brett one of his rare half smiles which disappeared as quickly as it had begun.

"Certainly, they will indeed suspect a trap. That's why they waited two days to retrieve the formula from the bank--they had to be sure it was not being watched and no police were around. However, if I know this James

Gang as well as I think I do, then their greed will be their undoing."

Brett sighed and rubbed the sleep out of his eyes. The guilt of his suspicion as to who was behind the James Gang has been eating away at him, this caused the nightmares of the last two nights, which were a mixture of South Africa and Danny.

Watson placed a reassuring hand on Brett's shoulder. He had come to be concerned for Brett both as a doctor and out of respect for his military past. Watson knew Brett had held back far more than he revealed to Watson when they were waiting for Holmes to return from the Richmond Hotel. He knew that Brett needed the support of a friend, particularly now. *Not unlike myself, back when I first met Holmes,* Watson thought. *Alone, recovering, and trying to put the war behind me. Had I not met Holmes and been supported by him I don't know how well I would have coped on my own.* Remembering his own nightmares, Watson clenched his jaw. He did not want to lose Holmes and would do anything to prevent that from happening. Holmes broke into his thoughts,

"Watson, we must be ready for a long night ahead of us. Once the James Gang has the formula, it will only take them a few hours to make the new explosives, as Mr Sullivan can confirm. They will strike immediately, as their plans are ready to be put into operation, and have been since the very beginning of this case."

"Yes, you are correct, Mr Holmes," agreed Brett, "there is not much to it really, and the process is relatively quick."

Watson went over to his desk, took out his revolver and started to load it. He felt the revolver shake in his hand and fought down the fears that had haunted him in the last few days. He had to be strong not only for himself but to protect Holmes as well. He closed the revolver barrel with a sharp click and held onto it firmly. He looked up at Holmes, who was studying him intently.
"When do we leave, Holmes?" asked Watson, hoping Holmes had not noticed his momentary lapse.

Holmes considered Watson's questions and furrowed his eyebrows; he was seriously concerned about Watson. Holmes had heard Watson screaming in his sleep over the last two days and had entered Watson's bedroom more than once to lay a reassuring hand on his shoulder. The revolver shaking in Watson's hands only to served to confirm Holmes's worries. *But if I know my Watson, he will not let his own fears endanger the task ahead of us, and it would not be the same without him at my side.*

"We can leave in ten minutes, Watson, if you and Mr Sullivan care for a change of scene. I thought a meal for the three of us at Simpson's would be a pleasant way of passing the late afternoon before heading down to the vaults to face the James Gang," replied Holmes.

Watson smiled and agreed to the idea immediately; both Holmes and Watson looked to Brett for his consent.

Brett was surprised and moved by the invitation. It would be good to have a bit of normality in what had been a distressing few days.

"I'd be delighted to join you both, thank you," replied Brett.

With the matter settled, the trio put on their coats and walked out of the house and down Baker Street, soon arriving at the restaurant. A waiter showed them over to a table by and it was not long before they were enjoying their meals. As Brett watched Holmes and Watson talking, his mind drifted back to earlier, happier times. When he and Danny were discharged from the hospital after their return from South Africa, their first act was to celebrate by visiting the Criterion restaurant and sharing a bottle of champagne. Much laughter followed as Danny and Brett enjoyed the bonds of friendship. He would never have that again. *I will make the fiend behind all of this pay for what he did,* thought Brett, his eyes darkening with suppressed rage.

Holmes turned to his client and saw the look of anger in his eyes. Although Holmes had not known his client for long, he could sympathise with Brett, who had suffered two bereavements in so little time. Brett had a right to be angry. Holmes looked down at his watch, and then glanced at the window. It was past six o'clock and growing dark outside--time to make the journey to the bank and stand watch in the vaults. Seeing that everyone had finished, he paid the bill, and the small party made their way to a waiting cab, which took them to the bank.

Each man was alone with their thoughts during this time. They all knew of the danger ahead of them.

On arrival at the bank, they entered through a discreet side door. Mr Summers, the bank manager, to whom Holmes sent a telegram shortly after learning the formula had been collected by the James Gang, was there to greet them. He led them into the vaults, down the long winding staircase into the ever-increasing darkness, the only illumination coming from the lanterns he and Dr Watson carried. Quietly, they made their way to the vault that contained the gold bullion. The vault itself was impressive, finely decorated with the Bank of England's Seal of Arms. Brett looked at it with some sadness. *Such a shame for such a wonderful piece of work to be blown apart by greed, but still, this vault has been the cause of much lost blood.*

Summers said in a hushed voice, "Gentlemen, there is an adjoining room. If we wait there, we will not be seen by anyone, but we will be able to hear and observe anything that happens tonight—if anything *does* happen."

Summers still had doubts about Holmes's theory, but Holmes had saved the bank from embarrassment once before. It would be foolish to ignore his warning now.

"Thank you, Mr Summers, that is a capital plan," said Holmes, his eyes alight.

The party moved into the adjoining room and began their long vigil. An hour became two, then four.

Holmes began to worry that he had been wrong and there would be no robbery tonight as he looked at his watch and saw that it was almost two o'clock in the morning. He watched as Watson quietly stood up to stretch his leg, which had been wounded in the Afghan War. Suddenly, Watson tensed and quickly crouched down, placing his hand on Holmes's shoulder. Holmes gripped Watson's arm and they both silently edged forward. Brett cautiously followed behind, ignoring the protest from his still not healed ribs.

Holmes watched the intruders make their way into the vaults. They had inside help, Holmes realised, noticing that one of the intruders was wearing a bank security uniform. This had been meticulously planned. The three intruders opened a bag, carefully lifted out a box and opened the lid. Holmes saw that the box indeed contained gelignite--a dozen wet-looking sticks wrapped together with sticky tape and attached to a container with a yellowish substance. One of the thieves moved forward and began to attach the explosives to the vault doors. The bank security guard was now keeping watch at the entrance through which they had come in, not suspecting there was an adjoining room. Instead of guarding the bank, he was now guarding a crime being committed. The second thief watched the explosives being put on the door. Holmes nodded to Watson, indicating now was the time to act, before the fuse was lit. Watson drew his revolver, and Holmes and Watson sprang out from their hiding place.

"Stop right there!" shouted Holmes.

The bank guard swung round in surprise on hearing Holmes, instantly recovered, and, with an angry cry, hit out at the nearest person to him. Watson saw the attack coming and raised his arms to protect himself from the blow. But the guard was too strong and Watson was flung back onto the floor, hitting it hard and dropping his revolver, which skidded across floor. Watson got up groggily, but not before his attacker lashed out again, hitting him in the stomach this time. Watson doubled over in pain.

Holmes was busy fending off his own attacker and had successfully dispatched him, landing a heavy blow which sent him sprawling. He turned to see Watson doubling over and was aghast.

"Watson!" cried Holmes, who rushed to Watson's side, broke his fall, and dispatched his attacker in one swift motion with a hard left hook. Brett had been watching the action. He saw the third thief coming from behind Holmes, about to lunge at him. Brett saw Watson's revolver on the floor, quickly snatched it up and pointed it at the thief's head.

"Don't even think about it!" said Brett, glaring at the thief. He pressed the gun harder against the thief's head for good measure.

Brett looked back at Holmes, who was helping Watson up. He was relieved to see that they were both all right, although Watson was leaning heavily against Holmes, clearly in some discomfort.

"Well done, Mr Sullivan!" cried Holmes as he pushed the remaining two thieves into a corner. Taking the cue, Brett did the same with the third thief. The three of them looked a sorry sight, nursing cuts and bruises. Brett bent down to examine the explosives, carefully defused them, and placed them back in the box. He let out a deep sigh when he closed the lid and the danger of the explosives accidentally going off was over. They heard the sound of several feet clambering down the stairs and then saw a familiar face enter the vault.

"Ah, Inspector Lestrade! Good of you to join us, you have excelled yourself tonight in catching three thieves in the act of committing a daring robbery. I congratulate you, sir."

Lestrade turned to his constables, instructed them to handcuff the thieves, and then turned back to Holmes.

"Thank you for your assistance, Mr Holmes. It is greatly appreciated. Well, I'd best be going back to the Yard and getting these ruffians under lock and key. Are you coming down with us?"

Holmes smiled. It was so typical of Lestrade to quickly claim the credit but at least justice had been served tonight.

"No, Lestrade, I think tonight's activities have exhausted us all," replied Holmes.

"Good night then, Mr Holmes, and thank you."

Lestrade escorted the thieves out with the help of his constables. He was looking forward to the reception back at the Yard tonight for bringing in three would-be robbers of the Bank of England.

Mr Summers, who had come out of the adjoining room now that it was safe to do so, shook Holmes's hand.

"Well done, sir, well done! The bank will be generous with its fee to you for saving it once more."

Holmes waved the manager off. He would discuss payment later. His concern now was with Watson, nothing else mattered.
Brett followed Holmes and Watson out of the bank and into the street. They would have to walk a bit, for the nearest cab was further down the street. Brett did not mind; he needed to clear his head after an eventful night. Brett was also worried. It had been too easy, he thought. The James Gang had known it was a trap, so why did they put up so little resistance? It also bothered him that the head of the gang was still at large. Brett grew uneasy. Brett put his hands in his trouser pockets and felt the cold metal of the revolver in his hand. He had forgotten he still had the gun and was about to give it back to Holmes, when suddenly two men appeared in front of him. One of them held a club in his hand. Brett wasted no time and instantly leapt forward to tackle the club-wielding man. They both went down, but Brett found his opponent too strong, and as he got up again to

face the attacker, he felt a sharp kick in his ribs which sent him sprawling down to the pavement. He let out a cry of pain as he gasped for air.

Holmes started to move forward to help Brett up, but was halted in his tracks by a voice he had hoped never to hear again. His blood ran cold at the sound.

"For a dead man, you move too quickly, Holmes. I would not advise you to move now—that is, if you value your life."

Watson also recognised the voice. *No, it can't be, oh God, no,* thought Watson, shutting his eyes for a second as the nightmares of the past few nights came flooding back. This was the ghost that he had feared most. Only now it was no ghost--Watson opened his eyes and saw the robed figure move closer toward Holmes. The man pulled down his hood and smiled malevolently at Holmes and Watson as they stared in horror at his badly disfigured face; the grey eyes and long straggly hair, however, were unmistakable.

"Moriarty!" cried Watson, as he struggled to overcome his revulsion and fear of the man before him.

"Yes, Doctor, you thought I was dead. You were wrong. I climbed out of that watery abyss and survived. I spent months in pain thanks to your precious friend and now I will have my revenge at long last. Say goodbye again to your friend, Doctor,"
Moriarty quickly whisked out a gun and aimed at Holmes, pulling the trigger.

With a scream of "*No!*" Watson pushed Holmes out of the way as the gun fired. The impact caused Watson to jerk back and then to fall heavily to the ground. A crimson red patch began to form across his chest. A scream shattered the night.

"Watson!"

Chapter Twelve

"Watson!" cried Holmes as he saw Watson fall.

Holmes felt his legs give way as he fell to the ground next to Watson. He frantically searched for Watson's pulse and his chest tightened at being unable to find one, but then Holmes felt a hand squeezing his and looked into pain filled hazel eyes. Holmes swallowed past a lump in his throat and quickly tore open Watson's blood-covered shirt. He saw the bullet wound had dug deep into Watson's shoulder and had hit his collarbone. Holmes quickly took his scarf off and pressed it to the wound with shaking hands.

Watson groaned as the pressure increased the intensity of white-hot pain radiating through his shoulder and across his chest. His head was spinning badly. He had heard Holmes shout his name, but the sound seemed so distant. Watson fought to open his eyes. There was Holmes bending over him, a concerned look on his face.

"Holmes..." said Watson weakly, trying to reassure his friend, but his efforts only launched him into a painful coughing fit.

Holmes pushed Watson back down and whispered,

"Watson, don't try to talk, just lie still, my friend."

Watson clutched Holmes's arm and sagged back against Holmes; the effort of trying to speak had exhausted him.

Holding Watson in his arms, Holmes spun his head round and faced Moriarty, full of rage. If looks could kill, Moriarty would have been dead as Holmes's steel-grey eyes bored into the eyes of his nemesis.

"How very touching I'm sure," said Moriarty. "Not the result I had been planning but effective all the same. Your weakness will be your downfall."

Holmes gently laid Watson down and stood up, replying vehemently,

"Go to hell! You should have died at Reichenbach Falls, but you will not survive this night, I promise you that!"

Moriarty laughed chillingly, his eyes shining with an insane zeal.

"Oh come now, Holmes, I have already survived hell, thanks to you, when I spent hours crawling out of that watery abyss. You forget I am armed, and I will see you die, but not before I see you suffer the same pain I did before."

Holmes stepped forward but was forced to stop short when he heard a bang and felt searing pain as the bullet slammed against his leg. Clutching his leg with a groan, he fell backwards, almost crashing down on Watson.

Watson, still struggling to overcome his own pain, gasped as Holmes fell. Ignoring his own injury, Watson inched his way closer to Holmes and grabbed his arm, calling his name in an unsteady voice.

"Holmes!"

Holmes bit back the pain and turned to face Watson, who was shaking, his face ghostly white. Holmes slumped back against a wall and gripped Watson's arm, trying to reassure him.

"It's all right, Watson, I'm all right."

Moriarty towered over them both with his gun raised. Holmes and Watson looked at each other, fearing that the end for them both was close. Watson felt himself sinking as the impact of his wound drained his strength. As he fought against the blackness that was threatening to overwhelm him, Watson said,

"I did not think it would end like this, forgive me, Holmes."

As Watson felt himself slipping away, he thought he heard Holmes's distant reply,

"I'm sorry I let you down, Watson, my very dear friend."

Holmes held tightly onto Watson, who was now lying slumped against him unconscious. He looked up and faced the barrel of a gun pointing right at him. *At least Watson won't have to see this,* thought Holmes as he closed his eyes and braced himself for the bullet he knew would kill him.

Brett had been watching in horror as Moriarty fired his gun and Watson fell. With a snarl of rage, Brett picked himself off the ground and faced his attacker, striking out a hard blow across his jaw which sent him flying back and landing hard against a pile of sandbags stacked up near a wall. Brett's attacker came up again, but Brett was ready and landed another heavy blow into the rib cage of his attacker, and the attacker stumbled backwards. Brett grabbed the man by the collar and raised Watson's revolver, hitting his attacker across the head. The blow rendered his attacker unconscious. Brett stood up; the fight had exhausted him and he clutched his side, as his ribs stabbed at him painfully.

He staggered up the street, but not before he heard another gunshot and saw Holmes fall. Brett stumbled forward, his hand tightening around Watson's revolver. Enraged by what he saw, he and cried out angrily, "Don't you dare do it, you murdering fiend!"

Both Holmes and Moriarty looked up in the direction of the voice and saw a figure stumble forward, pointing Watson's revolver straight at Moriarty.

Moriarty stared at Brett and then, recovering from the shock of being interrupted, remarked drily,

"Ah, Mr Sullivan, what an unexpected surprise!"

Brett stared in anger and repulsion at this disfigured evil man. He remembered the day when he and Danny had been clearing out his cousin's office after his murder and discovering a document that had led him to suspect who was behind the James Gang. It was a contract agreement, but what had drawn the attention of Brett was the signature. It was signed by Moriarty himself under his real name. Moriarty had made the fatal mistake of supposing that he would not be found out by someone working in such a small firm, in a backwater place, away from London and Sherlock Holmes. However, Moriarty had not gambled on the fact that Brett had spent his convalescence in the hospital reading *The Strand Magazine* and was all too well aware of the events that had taken place in Switzerland. Seeing the name had made Brett's blood run cold.

"You are responsible for the murder of my cousin and of my closest friend, you miserable excuse for a human being!" raged Brett.

Moriarty spat back, "Do you think I care anything for that?! You have no proof and you are just someone in the way whom I can crush easily. My man can easily do that," said Moriarty, looking around for the man in question.

"I don't think your man will help you any more tonight, as he is quite unconscious. As to proof…I didn't tell anyone about the document I found that connected you to all of this. Not even Mr Holmes, for I could not be entirely sure. I have kept it safe in another deposit box at another bank. Unfortunately, my suspicions were proved correct."

Brett kept his eyes trained on Moriarty while he spoke to Holmes, who was still holding Watson. "Forgive me for not telling you everything, I thought you would think I was mad. I felt very guilty about holding back, I really did. Will Dr Watson be all right?"

Holmes looked up at Brett with a newfound sense of respect. He smiled grimly.

"It's all right, Sullivan, you could not possibly have known it would end like this. But we do need to get Watson to the hospital as soon as possible."

Brett's face clearly showed a deep sense of appreciation at Holmes's words. Brett turned to face Moriarty again and a wave of sadness washed over him. There stood a man, badly disfigured, full of vindictive hatred, and, from what he had read in *The Strand Magazine,* a brilliant mind but used for evil purposes. Now all Brett saw was a man bent only on revenge. Brett inhaled deeply and closed his eyes, *to kill Moriarty for what he has done would make me no better than he is.*

Brett lowered Watson's revolver and began to laugh from sheer relief, as the pain of the last year began to lift from his shoulders. *The hangman will take care of this fiend*, thought Brett.

Moriarty stared at Brett incredulously, not understanding what Brett had just done, and raged at him,

"Do not jest with me, sir, I mean to have my revenge."

Moriarty lifted his gun, pointed it at Holmes and pulled back the trigger. This time Brett did not hesitate. He squeezed the trigger on Watson's revolver and fired. Moriarty looked down at his shoulder and back up at Brett in shocked surprise, clutching his shoulder in pain. His gun fell to the floor; the metallic sound reverberated around the cobbled street as it hit the ground.

"You shot me, you, of all the people I..."

"You forget, sir, I am a soldier," said Brett grimly.

Brett fired again as Moriarty lunged forward, his eyes wild as he tried to grab Brett by the neck. Moriarty staggered back as the bullet hit him squarely in his chest, a red stain already spreading across shirt front. Moriarty dropped to his knees and then rolled sideways to the ground. Blood poured from his mouth and he gurgled, choking on his own blood. The gurgling became quieter and quieter and then ceased. Moriarty's eyes remained wide open, seemingly staring blankly at Brett who stood over Moriarty, holding Watson's still-smouldering revolver.

Brett dropped the revolver to the ground and collapsed to his knees, his whole frame trembling. He had killed the man responsible for Danny's and Matthew's deaths. Brett bowed his head. A great weight had been lifted from his shoulders. He was free. It was finally over. Moriarty was dead.

Chapter Thirteen

Holmes stared in shock at the crumpled form of Professor Moriarty; it took him a moment to finally register that--at last--his arch enemy was dead. He turned back to Watson; the scarf he had pressed down on Watson's wound was now soaked in blood. Holmes placed his hand on Watson's forehead, noting with alarm that it was cold and clammy. He felt for Watson's pulse and found it to be shallow and fast. He needed to get Watson to hospital immediately. Holmes tried to stand up but let out a cry of agony from the pain in injured leg, falling back down again next to Watson.

Holmes's cry of agony cut through to Brett, who was still trembling. Brett stood up and stumbled forward over to Holmes and Watson. He knelt down beside Watson and looked up at Holmes. Holmes spoke first,

"We must get him medical attention--he has lost a great deal of blood, but I cannot walk. Can you fetch a cab?"

Brett nodded but first he bent to examine Watson's injury. He had trained as a field medic whilst in South Africa. Brett carefully lifted the scarf off Watson's shoulder and saw that it was not a superficial wound-- the bullet had penetrated deep into Watson's shoulder. Brett placed his hand carefully over the wound, probing further. Treating this would require a skilled surgeon, he could do very little. Brett took off his jacket and removed his shirt. He tore the shirt into strips and used them to carefully dress Watson's wound. It would slow the bleeding down for the time being.

Holmes had looked at Brett in astonishment and then with respect.

"How bad is it?" asked Holmes, his grey eyes clouded with worry.

Brett looked up as he was tying the last knot in the improvised bandage.

"I'd be lying, Mr Holmes, if I said that it was not serious. Keep him warm whilst I go and get help. I will try not to be long."

Brett gently placed his jacket on Watson and stood up, swaying as he did so. Brett fought back his own pain knowing that Holmes and Watson were now relying on him. With one final look at both Holmes and Watson, Brett broke into a light sprint down to the end of the street and into the next.

It was not until a few streets later that Brett found a lone cab parked outside a house. Brett drew a ragged breath in relief as he saw the cab. The cab was unattended while the driver was helping an elderly couple with their luggage as they made their way down their front steps. Brett looked apologetically at the couple as he climbed onto the driver's seat and took the reins. He was going to commandeer the cab and nothing was going to stop him.

"I'm sorry," said Brett, "but I have a medical emergency and I need to get two injured people to hospital as fast as I can. I'll make sure this cab is returned to you as soon as possible, driver."

Without waiting for a reply, Brett whipped the horse and quickly sped back to Holmes and Watson.

Holmes clenched his jaw as the pain in his leg worsened. But Holmes was not concerned about that. He looked down at his friend and held on to him tightly. Watson had been so worried in these past few days and now he is lying here badly injured. It had been ten minutes since Brett left to get help and Holmes hoped it would not be much longer. He suddenly felt Watson go limp in his arms. Holmes gripped Watson's good shoulder, quickly reaching for a pulse and finding it very weak. He shouted,

"Hold on, Watson, I can't lose you now. Don't you dare leave me! Watson!"

Holmes's voice broke; he placed his head in his hands berating himself for leading Watson into danger. He felt a hand on his arm and looked up to see Watson's pain-filled hazel eyes staring at him.

"Holmes…I'm here…" Watson stopped short, overcome by the pain, and let out a groan. "Not your fault Holmes...I could not let him kill you..."

Watson gasped again and felt the twirls of blackness encroach on him again; the effort of speaking had exhausted him. Holmes pressed Watson's hand and spoke softly,

"Watson, it's all right, rest now, my friend."

Watson struggled to say something more to Holmes but found he could not, his eyes grew heavier and he succumbed to the blackness once more. Holmes's eyes filled with tears as he watched his friend fighting valiantly to stay awake but ultimately losing the battle. And then he heard the most welcome sound he could possibly have wished for, horse's hooves approaching ever closer. Holmes looked up and sighed in relief as he saw Brett bringing the cab and horse to a halt. *Did Brett steal a cab?* thought Holmes in grim amusement as he watched Brett climb down from the carriage and run towards him.

Brett saw Holmes and Watson as he ran up to them and did not like what he saw. *Have I been away too long?* thought Brett as he once more knelt down beside Holmes and Watson and looked up at Holmes. Holmes responded to Brett's unspoken question,

"Watson came round a few moments ago, but he was in a great deal of pain. We must get him to a hospital quickly."

Brett carefully lifted Watson, carried him to the waiting cab, gently placed him inside and went back for Holmes. Holmes cried out as he stood once more on his injured leg, but Brett took most of Holmes's weight, half-carried him to the waiting cab, and helped him climb in. Brett saw the still form of Professor Moriarty and his face darkened in anger but he wasted no further time as he spun round and jumped back into the driver's seat. He had to get Holmes and Watson to a hospital quickly. He took grip of the reins and commanded the horse to break into a canter; the cab sped away into the London mist, racing to the nearest hospital. The journey to the Charing Cross Hospital took no longer than ten minutes and Brett stopped the cab directly outside the front entrance, yelling for help. A doctor and two nurses came running out and Brett instructed them to help the two injured passengers inside. He watched as the medical staff took charge and got Holmes and Watson inside. Relieved, Brett unsteadily climbed down from the driver's seat and leant back heavily against the cab, exhaustion washing over him. He suddenly felt the place beginning to spin and his legs giving way. As Brett collapsed to the ground, he felt a pair of strong hands break his fall before oblivion took over.

Chapter Fourteen

Dr Watson was staring into the lifeless eyes of his friend Sherlock Holmes. The grey eyes bored into him and Watson was clutching Holmes's body shouting his name. Moriarty had killed Holmes and was standing over him, gloating with the still-smouldering revolver in his hands. Watson and buried his face in his hands, calling for Holmes over and over again. And then he heard a voice calling to him.

"Watson!"

Watson shook his head, *Holmes was dead, it could not be...*

"Watson! Listen to me!"

Watson drew nearer to the commanding voice and saw Holmes standing before him, but Holmes was dead, this was impossible. Watson moved forward as Holmes called his name again.

"Watson! I'm right here! *Wake up!*"

Watson grabbed Holmes by the shoulders and suddenly opened his eyes, still disoriented. "Holmes?" asked Watson tentatively.

Holmes sat back, breathing a sigh of relief, but kept his hand on Watson's arm, and smiled at his friend.

"Thank heaven, Watson. You gave me rather a fright, old man."

Watson blinked and looked round the room. He had trouble remembering what had happened and how he got here. He groaned as he tried to sit up and the pain of his shoulder wound hit him with full force. He felt strong hands supporting him. Watson tried to talk again but could only manage a croak as the dryness of his throat caused him to cough. Holmes laid Watson back gently, poured a glass of water and then helped Watson sit back up. Watson accepted the glass gratefully with shaky hands and slowly drank the water, and on doing so fell back against Holmes in exhaustion. Suddenly, the events of the night came rushing back to Watson and he looked again at Holmes and for the first time saw Holmes's heavily bandaged leg.

"Holmes, you're hurt!"

Watson tried to sit up and reach for Holmes, but the sudden movement only served to jar Watson's shoulder even further and Watson choked back a cry of pain.

Holmes started forward and pushed Watson back down onto his bed.

"Watson, for goodness' sake, take it easy! I'm all right. You've been in hospital for two days suffering from a mild fever but you will be all right now. But overexerting yourself will not help you one bit!" snapped Holmes, whose exhaustion from keeping a vigil over Watson was beginning to show.

Watson lay back, looking at Holmes intently; he noticed the dark rings under Holmes's eyes and remembered the events of two nights ago. Watson shivered. His worst nightmares nearly came true. *If it had not been for Brett Sullivan, we wouldn't be here now,* mused Watson. *What has happened to him anyway?*

"Holmes, what happened to Brett Sullivan? Is he all right?"

Holmes told Watson how Brett had killed Moriarty and gone for help, successfully bringing them to the hospital.

"He is all right. He collapsed on arriving here, due to exhaustion and concussion. He was discharged yesterday and is now back at the Richmond Hotel. He was greatly concerned about you, however, and did look in on you several times."

Relieved that Brett was unharmed, Watson smiled and looked back at Holmes, eyeing his bandaged leg again with concern.

"How is your leg, Holmes?"

"It's much better now, Watson. The bullet did not shatter any bones and was easily removed. I too was discharged yesterday, but I could not leave you alone here."

Watson tiredly reached out, found Holmes's arm, and squeezed it.

"Thank you, Holmes. When was the last time you slept? I suspect it has been a while ago. You should go get some sleep now, I'll be fine."

Holmes looked up at Watson with a twinkle in his eyes. *My friend the doctor, always thinking of others and not himself. I came so close to losing him.* Holmes saw Watson's exhaustion.

"Don't worry about me, Watson; it is you who needs rest. Sleep now and when you wake up I'll be here."

Watson smiled gratefully and closed his eyes. And for the first time in many nights, Watson was not haunted by his nightmares.

Holmes looked down at his friend fondly. It had been a difficult and painful case, but all was right once more. Together they would help each other overcome the physical and emotional pain. He would never leave Watson and Holmes knew Watson would never leave him. Their bodies may be broken, but their friendship would always be unbreakable. Holmes sat back and closed his eyes, which were growing heavier by the minute. His last thoughts before he fell asleep were of how privileged he was to have such a close friend as Watson. As the two friends slept, the only sound in the room was the gentle breeze of the wind outside. Time would move on and the world would change, but the two friends would always remain together to fight injustice and to be a shining beacon in a world that was becoming ever darker and more dangerous.

Epilogue

One Month Later

Brett Sullivan caught his breath after the long strenuous climb. The autumn wind chilled him and he wrapped his overcoat tighter round him. He closed his eyes as he listened to the gushing water below. Coming back here was very difficult, but he knew he had to. Opening his eyes, he surveyed the scene around him. Lodore Falls. *Where it all started and is now ending,* thought Brett. He picked up the urn he had placed beside him and clutched it tightly. The urn held all that remained of Danny Peterson.

Brett choked back tears as he looked at the urn. He had brought Danny home. Brett carefully unscrewed the top of the urn and gently scattered its contents over the Falls until nothing remained. Brett lowered the urn and let it slip out of his hands and fall to the ground. He stood rigidly, staring into the Falls, tears streaming down his face. It was over now. He was alone. Everyone he knew was dead. Just then, however, he felt a firm hand squeeze his shoulder.

Brett turned to see the reassuring face of Dr Watson, with Sherlock Holmes standing beside him. They both travelled to the Lake District to accompany Brett back home, but decided to stay in the area for a few days to convalesce. Brett said, "Thank you both for coming. You did not have to do this."

Watson smiled, "It was the least we could do, after you saved our lives back in London. Holmes and I will never forget that."

Holmes's grey eyes shone as he looked at Brett.

"Watson is, of course, right. We could not abandon a friend in his time of need. If you ever need us again, you know where to find us. But I would hope that you visit us from time to time in any case; your presence at Baker Street would be most welcome."

Watson nodded in agreement and continued, "What will you do now?"

Brett looked at both Holmes and Watson, moved by their kind words and honoured that they considered him a friend.

"Well, I am selling the business. I don't think I could stand to work there anymore; too many memories. However, I am going to start a new business, one of which I hope you will approve."

"What will that be?" asked Watson eagerly.

Brett's eyes twinkled mischievously.

"I am going to open a new detective agency here in the Lake District, to take on cases of my own. The last year has taught me many things and with my past military experience I think it would be something I would enjoy!"

"Ha! That is a capital idea! " cried Holmes, breaking into a fit of laughter and slapping Brett on the back affectionately.

Grinning, Watson shook Brett's hand.

"And the very best of luck to you, sir! We both wish you success."

Brett smiled as he watched the duo walk away, allowing him time on his own to take one final look around the Falls.

Brett inhaled deeply and listened to the sound of the Falls. He sensed a new beginning unfolding. He also knew that he would see Holmes and Watson again someday. Although Matthew and Danny were now dead, he would never be alone with Holmes and Watson as friends. An inner glow of warmth spread through him and Brett smiled, then turned and walked away into the morning mist, leaving behind an important chapter in his life but embarking on an exciting new journey.

As Brett walked away, two figures emerged from the Falls and watched. They looked at each other and smiled.

"Will he be all right?" one asked the other.

"He will be now, my friend. And we will be with him by his side forever, to catch him if he falls."

The two figures faded away, lost in the ever flowing waterfall. All that remained was the eternal sound of the gushing Falls, and of the birds singing in the trees. Peace had descended on Lodore Falls once more.

The Call Of Angels

Heap on the wood!--the wind is chill; But let it whistle as it will; we'll keep our Christmas merry still.

(Sir Walter Scott)

Watson

The snow was falling heavily and Dr Watson pulled up his coat collar, trying to keep out the freezing air. It had been a long day in surgery treating patient after patient with the current outbreak of flu. There had been so many patients that afternoon soon became early evening, and the last patient did not leave until almost seven o'clock that night. Watson sighed and leant heavily on his walking stick, exhaustion getting the better of him. He had missed the last cab that would have taken him back home to Baker Street. Cab stands, along with all other businesses, were closing up for Christmas Eve. He would have to walk home instead. Watson closed the front door of his surgery behind him and walked slowly down the steps and into the snowy night. He did not mind the snow, but he hated the ice and knew he would have to be careful walking home in this weather. *I hope I get home in time to give Holmes his present*, thought Watson. He smiled fondly as he thought of his friend. Holmes never cared for Christmas much but he knew that they both welcomed each other's company, especially now. Watson grinned in anticipation of Holmes's surprise at the present Watson had bought him. *He may be the world's only consulting detective but even he can't be anticipating the surprise I have for him.* Watson laughed softly as he began walking down the street, the wintry snow soon engulfing him.

Holmes

Sherlock Holmes sat in his chair, warily looking around the sitting room. Mrs Hudson had been busy decorating the place with tinsel and holly to "give the place some festive spirit". *How can my clients expect me to act in a businesslike manner if the agency looks like something out of Dickens' Christmas Carol!* moodily thought Holmes. He got up, went over to his Persian slipper, took out some tobacco and stuffed it into his favourite pipe, a present Watson gave him the previous Christmas. The fact was not lost on Holmes as he glanced down at his pipe for a moment, his lips curled up into a half smile which vanished as soon as it had appeared. Holmes lit his pipe, sank back into his chair, and soon the room was shrouded in smoke. *Mrs Hudson would not approve of her festive efforts being obscured,* thought Holmes with some amusement. But Holmes's amusement soon turned to worry as he looked at his pocket watch and saw that it was seven past the hour. Watson was late. Where was he? Holmes hoped Watson had managed to catch the last cab back to Baker Street. Getting up from his chair, Holmes looked out of the window and saw that it was snowing heavily. Watson would never survive walking in this treacherous environment. Holmes decided to wait another half an hour. If Watson was not home by then, he would go and search for him. It may be Christmas Eve but the dangers of walking alone in the streets of London were never far away. Holmes rubbed his side where he had been stabbed just over a fortnight ago. Holmes recalled the details of the case as he gazed out the window. He had been pursuing the Aldywich Butcher; the reason for his name was the state of the bodies he had left behind. If not for Watson and Lestrade, Holmes would have become the next victim. They bravely fought off the attacker, but Holmes did not escape unscathed. Although the wound was healing now, Watson had ordered him to rest as much as possible--an order he feared he would now have to countermand.

Watson

Watson wrapped his scarf and coat tighter round him and grimaced as he tried to shield himself from icy wind and the snow, which was falling heavier and heavier. Watson closed his eyes as a sharp pain shot up his leg. Watson leant tiredly against a wall and brought out his pocket watch. It was almost eight o clock. It should have taken approximately an hour to get back to Baker Street, but he was only a quarter of the way there and an hour had already passed. *Holmes would be wondering where I am by now. He is exhausted enough without having to think about my whereabouts. To think I almost lost him almost two weeks ago.* Watson kept walking down the street, each step becoming more and more difficult as the cold really began to bite. Watson coughed and felt exhaustion tugging away at his dwindling reserves of energy. He had to go on. He could not give up now. Watson looked up and saw Hyde Park. He knew it well--it was a shortcut back to Baker Street. *If I walk through the park I could be back in*

Baker Street within half an hour! Watson crossed the road and opened the park gate. He knew it would not be closed for another two hours, giving him ample time to get across the park. The surge of excitement gave Watson renewed energy and he walked on, ignoring the snow and wind. He wanted nothing more than be sitting in front of the fire opposite Holmes, watching him open his Christmas present. Lost in his thoughts, Watson did not notice the patch of ice ahead of him until it was too late. Watson slipped and let out a cry as he crashed heavily to the ground, hitting his shoulder and his head. He lay in the snow face down, unmoving, unconscious, and alone.

Holmes

Holmes had been pacing in the sitting room for the last half hour. It was now nearly half past eight and Watson had not come home. He would wait no more. Holmes got his coat from his bedroom, quickly walked down the stairs, took his walking stick from the coat rack, and closed the front door behind him. Holmes quickly crossed the streets and headed towards Kensington, ignoring the pain in his injured side. It was indeed a cold night and Holmes was glad he had chosen to wear his ulster. Holmes shuddered more from fear of what may have happened to Watson than from the cold. Holmes stopped and rubbed the tiredness out of his eyes. *I cannot let my emotions get the better of me. I need to think clearly for Watson's sake. What route would he use to get back to Baker Street? In this weather his leg and shoulder are bound to be affected which would slow him down. He would be*

contemplating the quickest route back home. Of course!
Hyde Park! Holmes quickly headed in the direction of
Hyde Park, ignoring the increasing ferocity of the
snowfall. He had to get to Watson, no matter what the
weather!

Watson

 Slowly, Watson fought his way back to consciousness,
overcoming the blackness that had engulfed him. He
strained to hear a voice calling to him but could not
quite make it out.

"Holmes, is that you, old chap?" asked Watson in a
dazed voice.

Watson tried to focus on the voice, and as his mind
became clearer, he realised the voice belonged to
someone other than Holmes. Watson struggled to free
himself from the strong hands that were holding him
down, fearing he was being attacked.

"It's all right, Doctor, I will not harm you but you must
lie still. You have a nasty head injury and you have
badly bruised your shoulder in the fall and. I think your
leg is hurt too."

Watson opened his eyes and saw a man come into view.
He was in his early thirties and had blond hair and
piercing deep blue eyes. Watson was transfixed by the
sight at first and tried to raise himself but then fell back
with a moan as dizziness claimed him.

"Who are you?" asked Watson.

"My name is Gavri'el. I am the caretaker. I found you lying in the snow. But you are safe now."

Watson took stock of his surroundings. He was lying on a park bench, it was still snowing and he should be shivering but surprisingly was not. If this was this caretaker's idea of "safe", then he was in trouble. *Wait a minute, how did this man know I was a doctor?* he wondered, his sense of unease quickly returning.

"Thank you for rescuing me, Gavri'el, but how did you know I was a Doctor? I have never met you before!"

Smiling, Gavri'el replied, "Your occupation was not difficult to determine. Your hands are those of a surgeon, they are well scrubbed, and the smell of disinfectant is a further indication of your medical profession. You carry a walking stick embossed with the initials MVM, which can only stand for the University of Edinburgh College of Medicine and Veterinary Medicine."

Watson groaned and sank further back against the improvised pillow that lay under his head.

"You should meet Holmes, he would find a keen observer such as yourself to be of great interest," said Watson dryly.

"I should very much like to meet your friend someday, Doctor, but not tonight. However, I shall wait with you until he arrives."

Watson looked at Gavri'el, puzzled by the last remark, and shook his head. This caretaker was strange but he did not appear to present any danger.

"Gavri'el, I have to get back to my home. I am already late as it is. If you could just help me get up I'll be on my way."

Gently but firmly, Gavri'el pushed Watson back down.

"It is all right Doctor; Mr Holmes is coming and will be with you soon. You need to rest. You need not worry about your friend; he will be fine."

Watson felt his head throbbing anew and frowned in confusion at the words coming from this caretaker.

"What do you know of Holmes? Who are you?" asked Watson as some of the fear crept back into his voice.

Gavri'el smiled but it was a melancholy smile.

"Doctor, I have been watching you for a long time. You have suffered much but have found comfort and joy in your friendship with Holmes. I know you are concerned for his well-being at the moment. You will both be reunited shortly, but make the most of the reunion for the time is coming when you will face an event that will test the your friendship to the limit and you will suffer once more, although things will work out for the best in the long run."

Watson bolted upwards from his seat at these words, ignoring the almost overwhelming throbbing in his head.

"Just what do you mean by those remarks, sir?!" Watson was now regretting his decision to take a shortcut through this park. After tonight, he doubted he would ever walk through this park again.

Gavri'el shook his head and stood up, looking down at Watson and then glancing up as he heard the sound of approaching footsteps. "I must go; your friend is coming for you. You will be safe now. I have enjoyed meeting you at last. Goodbye, Doctor. We shall meet again one day."

Gavri'el turned to leave and Watson called out,

"But wait, you saved me tonight; I would like to thank you. And I'm certain that Holmes would too."

Gavri'el turned around, his blue eyes shimmering brightly.

"Dr Watson, you have already thanked me by helping so many souls in distress, especially on this particular night, even though you weren't quite well yourself. It was my turn to help *you* for a change. Have a good Christmas with Holmes, Doctor, and remember what I told you. Change is coming and you must prepare for that. I must go now, but I will be watching you."

And with these words Gavri'el walked away into the night and Watson could not be sure but he thought he saw Gavri'el disappear out of existence.

Watson shook his head and tried to get up but once more his injuries prevented him from doing so and he collapsed back against the park bench, groaning with the pain and beginning to shiver once more. Watson closed his eyes as they became heavier and heavier, exhaustion was claiming him once more but not before he heard a familiar voice shout out his name.

"Watson!"

Watson opened his eyes groggily and saw a familiar wiry figure running towards him. He managed to call out for Holmes before succumbing once more to the velvet veil of unconsciousness.

Holmes

The walk to Hyde Park was not easy. Holmes felt his side hurt more and more, *Watson had not been joking when he advised I should rest, as always with medical matters, he was, of course, right. I am still not ready to be loose on the streets of London, but I must not fail Watson now!* Holmes had been walking in the snowfall for almost an hour now and he leant heavily against a street lamp for a moment to catch his breath. He looked up and saw Hyde Park in front of him. Holmes made his way to the park entrance and looked round. He knew Watson had to be in Hyde Park, but where? His thoughts were interrupted by the sound of a voice addressing him.

"Can I help you, sir?"

Holmes spun round and came face to face with a tall man, his face and figure obscured by a hooded cloak.

"Yes, I am looking for a friend, he is lost in the snow here in Hyde Park. I am concerned he may also be hurt. Can you assist me?"

The tall man looked at Holmes and smiled.

Holmes looked back at the man. Usually he could deduce everything about a person from the start, but for some reason he could not ascertain who this man was, except for his magnetic blue eyes. *How odd*, thought Holmes. For the second time Holmes's train of thoughts was interrupted.

"Yes, I saw a gentleman earlier sitting on a park bench; if you go down this path here you should reach your friend in no time at all."

Holmes thanked the man and sprinted off down the path, ignoring the burning pain in his side. As the park bench came into view, he saw a familiar figure struggling to get up and falling back in pain.

"Watson!" cried Homes as he dashed forward and caught Watson before he fell back completely against the park bench.

Watson suddenly went limp in Holmes's arms; alarmed, Holmes checked for Watson's pulse, and, to his profound relief found it weak, but steady. Holmes took off his ulster and wrapped it around Watson. *He needs it more than I do; he is frozen and needs all the warmth he can get.*

"Oh my dear Watson," sighed Holmes, "what have you done to yourself? Let's get you home."

Carefully Holmes picked Watson up and carried him back to the entrance. Holmes was dreading the walk home, but to his surprise, he saw a cab waiting at the entrance.

"Evening, Guv, I was told to come here by a bloke, he was quite insistent too. Said he was a friend of yours. Anyway he said you needed a ride back to Baker Street. So if you kindly step inside, the sooner we get there and then I can get back to my wife who is waiting for me at home and wants me to pluck the turkey for tomorrow's Christmas dinner."

Holmes could not help chuckling at these words as he replied,

"Get us there as quickly as possible, and there will be five guineas in it for you."

Holmes looked down at his unconscious friend and his amusement turned to worry. He carefully stepped into the cab and placed Watson down next to him, holding onto him tightly. He tapped the roof to signal the cabbie to start his journey. As the horses gathered speed and headed back to Baker Street, Holmes looked down at his friend and said softly,

"I almost lost you tonight, Watson. What *were* you thinking?"

Tears formed in Holmes's eyes which Holmes angrily rubbed away with his sleeve and then held on to Watson tightly. Holmes would ensure this Christmas would be the best one they could share together.

Watson

The first sensation Watson felt as he once more came slowly round was the warmth. Not only that but a glowing warmth that enveloped him entirely. There was a familiar feel to it too. Watson opened his eyes and saw the flames of the coal fire flickering. The next thing he noticed was the afghan rug covering him and the familiar feel of a couch. Now he knew where he was. Home.

"Holmes, where are you?" croaked Watson.

"I am right here, old fellow. Take it easy, don't try to move. You banged yourself up badly last night but Dr Moore Agar was good enough to make a house call and tend to your injuries. You will be all right."

Watson broke an arm free of the afghan rug and placed his hand on Holmes's arm.

"Thank God you found me when you did, Holmes, I--"

Watson broke into a fit of coughing as his scratchy throat cut him off from speaking any further. Holmes got up and poured Watson a glass of water and came back, placing his arm behind Watson's shoulders and lifting his head to enable Watson to drink the water. Watson drank thirstily and quickly emptied the glass, leaning back heavily against Holmes.

Holmes gently placed some cushions behind Watson and helped Watson lie back.

"Rest, Watson, you are exhausted," said Holmes simply.

But Watson did not want to rest.

"Holmes, last night, did you meet anybody in the park?"

Surprised, Holmes looked up.

"Why yes, I did, Watson. He pointed me in your direction, lucky I bumped into him too as it could have taken me much longer to find you."

Watson nodded and regretted doing so as his head ached once more.

"What did he look like, Holmes?"

"Watson, what is the matter? He was just a man, tall, wearing a hooded cloak which obscured his face. Oddly enough, I could not deduce anything else about the man, but he saved both of us from being in the cold for much longer than we were."

"Holmes, last night, a man found me and waited with me until you arrived. Did you not see him?"

Holmes looked at Watson and wondered if the head injury were not more severe than Dr Agar had diagnosed.

"Watson, I did not see anyone else. Just yourself lying on the park bench. All I remember is being worried about getting you safely back home."

Watson absorbed this information, closed his eyes briefly, and then opened them again.

"Holmes, the person I saw was real. We talked, and some of what he said worried me. He spoke of us both as if he already knew us and warned me of danger to come. Holmes, I am worried about who it was I was talking to last night."

Watson once more gripped Holmes's arm and looked into his eyes.

Holmes realised Watson was serious about this. He decided to press Watson further on the matter.

"Did the man give his name? What else can you tell me?"

"He said he was the caretaker and gave his name as Gavri'el. He was tall, blond-haired, and the most piercing set of dark blue eyes you ever saw."

Holmes

Holmes stiffened at hearing Watson's description of the man who had come to Watson's rescue only a few hours earlier. It was very similar to the man he had encountered as well. And there was something familiar about the name too. Holmes got up and walked over to Watson's desk and gazed out of the window. It was now early Christmas morning. The snow had stopped falling at last and London was slowly waking up. Children were already in the street throwing snowballs at each other, laughing. Holmes smiled and remembered the time when he and Mycroft did the same, many years ago. Holmes turned to look down at Watson's desk and saw the row of books. *Florid romantic novels*, thought Holmes fondly. His eyes stopped at one particular book that stood out from the rest and he pulled it out from the shelf, surprised to find it amongst Watson's things.

"I did not realise you were a God-fearing man, Watson," said Holmes as he raised the said book in his hand walking back over to Watson.

"I'm not," said Watson laughing softly at Holmes's surprise. "It was given to me by my father and his father before him and so on, handed down through the ages. And now it is in my safekeeping."

Suddenly Watson paused and looked at Holmes intently, before finally coming to a decision.

"Keep it, Holmes, it's yours now, I'd like you to have it."

Holmes started to protest at this but Watson waved him off.

"Holmes, I don't have anyone else to give it to and you are the closest person I have to a brother anyway. I would like you to have it."

Holmes stared down at the book admiring the gold embossed title on the cover. He placed his hand on Watson's shoulder and squeezed it gently.

"Thank you, my dear Watson," said Holmes softly.

"You're welcome, old fellow. What time is it, Holmes?" asked Watson.

Holmes looked at his watch.

"Just after eight o'clock, Watson."

"Merry Christmas, Holmes!" exclaimed Watson excitedly. "I have a present for you, I hid it in the cabinet by the door before I went out yesterday morning. I'm afraid I am quite unable to fetch it now. You'll have to get it yourself."

Holmes smiled and walked over to the cabinet, laughing. He would never get Watson's limits; his Boswell was capable of surprising him at the most unexpected of times. Holmes opened the door of the cabinet and saw a parcel covered by red wrapping paper. He pulled the parcel out and carried it back over to Watson, setting it down on the floor before he disappeared into his bedroom to fetch his present for Watson, then came back and sat next to Watson, handing it to him.

"Go on, Holmes, you first!" said Watson playfully.

Holmes unwrapped his present to reveal the familiar outline of a case, thin at the top and bulging out at the bottom into a pear shape. He opened the lid of the case and gasped at the contents inside. Carefully he lifted it out of the case and stared at it in disbelief.

"Watson, you shouldn't have, this is a Stradivarius violin! Where did you find this?!"

Watson laughed.

"I found a music shop which had some offers on, I saw the violin and they were doing a special deal. I could not resist it, I knew your previous violin had been repaired several times over the last year and thought you might enjoy a new one."

"Thank you, my dear fellow."

Watson proceeded to unwrap his own present.

"Holmes, I don't believe it! This is wonderful, I have been after a new stationery set for some time and this is just what I needed. Thank you, Holmes."

Holmes got up and poured Watson a glass of mulled wine, handing it to him, then sitting back down next to Watson and quietly thinking.

Outside, the sound of children singing Christmas carols was starting up and Holmes frowned, not at the singing but at what Watson had told him earlier.

"Holmes, what is it?" asked Watson, concern now creeping into his voice.

"Watson, you said the name of the man who helped you last night was called Gavri'el. Well I have just remembered that name is an ancient Hebrew translation for the name of Gabriel. At the risk of sounding like one of your florid novels, Watson, I believe the man you saw last night was no man, but something much more than that."

Watson stared at Holmes and almost choked on his wine.

"Holmes, surely you are not implying that Gavri'el was actually Gabriel as in *the* Gabriel?!"

"Watson, when you have eliminated the impossible, whatever remains, however improbable, must be the truth."

Holmes had turned the pages of the book Watson had given him and found the illustration he had been looking for, handing the book to Watson.

Watson took a deep breath and looked up at Holmes.

"Holmes... surely, you don't mean to imply that the person who I spoke to last night was *the* Archangel Gabriel!"

Holmes's look never wavered.

"Yes, Watson, I do. And this is a story for which the world is not yet prepared. I am grateful he watched over you, Watson, for I would be lost without my Boswell."

Watson stared at Holmes and then heard the sound of the children singing. He leant back against the cushions taking in what Holmes had told him. He was becoming tired again and said sleepily to Holmes,

"Merry Christmas, old fellow."

Watson closed his eyes and the now-empty wineglass slipped from his hand. Holmes deftly caught the wineglass before it hit the floor and gently placed the afghan rug round Watson.

Holmes stood up and glanced up at the mantelpiece to the picture of the waterfalls that hung up overhead. He had been drawn more and more to this picture and he was unsure as to why. Holmes stared at the calendar on Watson's desk. It was December 25th 1890. Soon, it would be 1891. Holmes gazed fondly at his sleeping friend. He was determined, no matter what, to keep Watson close by him and never let him out of his sight. Last night had been such a close thing. Holmes sat down in his chair watching Watson and soon was overcome with sleep himself and fell into the arms of Morpheus. The Christmas carols from the street below filled the silent room.

A bright light shone into the room. Gabriel appeared and watched over the two sleeping friends. It would be a difficult year ahead for both of them, but they would never be alone.

The Adventure of the Wooden Boat

Chapter One: Shipwreck

Dr John Watson lay awake in his bed, staring at his ceiling of his room in Baker Street, troubled by the dream that had been plaguing him for the last three nights. His leg was hurting him and Watson rubbed it absent-mindedly. He closed his eyes, partly to shut out the pain shooting up his leg but also because he was replaying the dream in his mind. He had been just a young boy when he had run into his father's office crying that fateful afternoon, carrying the remains of a ship in a bottle that he had accidentally knocked off the mantelpiece and smashed as it crashed to the floor.

"Father, I am sorry, I broke you ship, I didn't mean to," said the young Watson, wiping away his tears with his sleeve.

His father looked up and saw the sobbing young boy standing in the middle of the study with the broken remains of the ship in the bottle.

"It's all right, John. I'm sure it was just an accident."

Watson's father bent down and helped his son pick up the broken glass and bits of wood that had dropped to his study floor.

Watson sat down and stared at the carpet, too ashamed to look at his father straight in the eye.

"John, would you like to help me make a new ship?" asked his father kindly.

John looked up at his father and his eyes shone brightly.

"Yes, please, Father, I would love to do that!" replied Watson, now looking at his father with anticipation.

His father laughed and placed his hand on his son's shoulder.

"Then we shall, my boy, and you will learn the secret of how to place the boat inside the bottle!"

A week later, Watson and his father were sitting down with the new boat they had made together.

"Well, John, it seems you have the hands of a surgeon. You should think about becoming one; you were very skilful in building that boat. Now, do you think you can put it in the bottle?"

John looked up at his father and smiled. He slowly pushed the boat into the bottle, pulled the thread attached to the boat trailing out of the bottle neck, and with a gentle tug raised the mast to a vertical position. "Bravo, John!" cried his father proudly.

Watson glowed with inner pride and then was surprised when his Father turned to him and said.

"John, you may keep that, I intended to give you the old ship in the bottle anyway. But I think this one is even more special because you made it yourself."

"Thank you, Father."

Only a month later, Watson's father was killed in a horrific railway accident. Watson cried for weeks afterwards. But he kept his promise. He became a surgeon and he kept his ship in the bottle.

Watson looked up at his dresser and picked up the ship in the bottle he had kept for all these years. He rubbed his eyes wearily and shook his head. *Why am I dreaming about what happened all of those years ago now?* Watson rose from his bed and walked over to his bedroom window. He watched the snow falling. It was only light snow for now but it would get heavier later on. He looked at his watch. It was almost nine o'clock in the morning. Watson could stand staying inside no longer. Bad leg or not, Watson was determined to go out for a walk and clear his head before the snow became too heavy. And as it was nearing Christmas anyway, Watson wanted to find something for Holmes as a present but he could not think what to get. *Maybe that task will distract me*, thought Watson. He dressed, put on his overcoat and walked out of the flat, closing the door behind him. Watson walked down Baker Street, determined to exorcise the ghosts that were haunting him.

Chapter Two: All At Sea

Dr Watson had spent the last two hours walking without focus or sense of purpose around the streets of London. The snow was beginning to fall heavier now; Watson felt the pain in his leg grow steadily worse and was relying more and more on his cane to help him move forward. Exhausted, Watson slumped against a shop window and wished that he had gone to Holmes to share his worries rather than find himself in this position. But pride and his need to spend time to himself had destroyed any chance of that. Watson was about to turn and call for a cab back to Baker Street when suddenly something caught his eye amongst the models displayed in the front window. Watson peered into the shop window and saw a large box with a picture of a French naval boat. He smiled. He knew that he would be housebound for the next week or so with his leg being so painful and it would not only be the perfect way to spend his time recovering but also make a wonderful Christmas present for Holmes! Watson dug into his pocket and brought out his wallet, looking at the price displayed next to the box. Satisfied that he had enough money, Watson limped into the shop and bought the model boat and necessary supplies. Watson left the shop with a lighter heart than when he had gone in. He limped heavily to a nearby waiting cab and instructed the driver to take him back to Baker Street.

Mrs Hudson met Watson as he walked back into the flat. She looked at Watson with concern, noting how tired and worn he looked.

"Dr Watson, we have been worried about you, especially after you left without saying good morning to Mr Holmes earlier."

Watson looked at Mrs Hudson guiltily. He had not meant to cause Mrs Hudson or Holmes any distress. He sighed, looking at the wrapped parcel and knew that he would not have a chance to do anything with his model boat for a few hours yet.

"Mrs Hudson, I'm going to put this in my room and I will join Holmes shortly."

Mrs Hudson smiled,

"Very good, sir, I'll let Mr Holmes know."

She watched with concern as Watson limped up the stairs. It was not like the Doctor to behave like this. *But at least he has Holmes, who will help him through whatever is troubling him*, she thought fondly. Mrs Hudson followed Watson up the stairs and relayed Watson's message to Holmes.

Holmes looked up at Mrs Hudson as she walked into the room. He had heard Watson's heavy footsteps a moment ago, noting Watson's limp with alarm.

"Mr Holmes, Dr Watson has arrived back home and will be joining you shortly. And if you don't mind me saying, he looked rather tired and I am very worried about him."

Holmes smiled reassuringly at his landlady, touched by her concern for his friend and colleague.

"Thank you, Mrs Hudson. Your concern is noted and I will endeavour to establish the cause of his current difficulties. Please do not distress yourself any further." Mrs Hudson smiled gratefully and left the room, quietly closing the door behind her. Holmes lit his pipe, filling it with tobacco from his Persian slipper, and sank back into his chair. He had heard Watson pacing in his room for the last few nights. Mrs Hudson's distress had only confirmed Holmes's concern. Holmes was determined to find out what was troubling his friend.

Chapter Three: Ship Building

Watson laid down his packages and took off his coat as he entered his bedroom. He was tired, somewhat hungry and in pain. The pain he could do something about. He went to his medical bag and took out a sachet of powder which he emptied into a glass filled with water. He gulped down the water and placed the glass down on his dresser. Watson left his bedroom and walked down the short flight of stairs to join Holmes in their shared sitting room. Watson tried to mask the pain in his leg as he walked into the sitting room and sat himself down in his chair by the fire. He knew Holmes would not be fooled, however. He drew closer into the fire, staring into it. The dream that had kept him awake these past few nights played over and over in his mind. Even the flames of the coal fire seemed to be mocking him as they flickered and wavered.

"Watson, I wonder if you would do me the kindness of reading to me this letter that came this morning," said Holmes, interrupting Watson's thoughts.
Watson looked up in surprise, not having fully registered what Holmes had said to him.

"I'm sorry, Holmes, a letter? What of it?" replied Watson trying to shake off the temporary disorientation caused by the interruption to his thoughts.

Holmes leant forward, handing Watson the letter.

"I want you to read it, my dear fellow," replied Holmes, his eyes betraying his deep sense of concern over

Watson's behaviour and appearance ever since he came into the room.

Watson took the letter and held back a sigh. He did not want to do this; he just wanted to be left alone. However, he could not hurt his friend by refusing his request. He cleared his throat and began to read the letter.

"Dear Mr Holmes:
I would be grateful if you could investigate the death of my father, which I believe to be murder. He was killed a week ago whilst travelling on business. They said it was an accident but my heart feels this was not the case. He would have never leant out of the train carriage door unless the train was stopped at a station. The Great Western Railway claimed that the train door was faulty, but I do not believe it is true. My father had no enemies that I know of but he did appear highly stressed before his death. I hope to hear from you at your earliest convenience.
Yours sincerely,
Paula Ashton."

Watson looked at the letter he had just finished reading to Holmes. All colour had drained from his face and the letter shook in his trembling hands. Watson had stood up when reading the letter, but now he felt his legs give way and he fell back into his chair. His chest tightened as he looked up at Holmes, his hazel eyes betraying his turmoil.

"Watson, what is it, my dear fellow?" asked Holmes, shocked by Watson's reaction to reading the letter out loud.

Watson stood up and gave the letter back to Holmes.

"I'm sorry Holmes, please excuse me. I am not myself and I will retire to bed. Good night, Holmes."

Without waiting for Holmes's response, Watson turned abruptly and left the room.

Holmes stared at the vacant seat, taking in what had happened. It took no powers of deduction that the contents of the letter had clearly upset his Boswell, *but why?* thought Holmes. Holmes jumped up from his seat, leapt over the couch and out of the room, and sprinted up the stairs to Watson's bedroom. He softly knocked on the door.

"Watson, please talk to me, what is wrong?"

Sitting on his bed, Watson listened to Holmes as he struggled to regain his composure, the letter had come too close to hitting home and he wiped away the tears that had fallen as he had left the sitting room. He did not want Holmes to see him like this.

"Holmes, please leave me alone. I don't wish to be disturbed, I'll see you in the morning".
Holmes was surprised and hurt by the curt response. *This was not like Watson*, he thought. *Something is seriously wrong and I mean to find out what it is.*

Holmes opened the door to Watson's bedroom and found Watson sitting on his bed. *He's been crying. Good grief , what were those parcels on his bed?* thought Holmes. He walked over to Watson and sat next to him on the bed, gently placing his hand on Watson's shoulder, offering silent support for his troubled friend.

Watson looked up at Holmes. By rights, he should be angered by Holmes's intrusion into his bedroom but one consequence of living with a great detective such as Holmes was that you could rarely keep a secret from him. Watson sighed. Holmes was his friend, no, not a friend, more like a brother. He had a right to know what was happening, and besides, friendship was about sharing as well as giving.

"Holmes, I'm sorry; I should not have run out like that. It's just that letter brought back some rather unpleasant memories that I've been dreaming of lately and I--"

Watson's voice cracked and he buried his face in his hands. Holmes laid his hand on Watson's arm and said quietly,

"It's all right, Watson, I'm here, please tell me about the dream. After all, you keep telling me that it is good to discuss these things."

Watson gave a half smile, nodding in agreement.

"Holmes, my father was killed in a railway accident when I was just a young boy. It left me greatly distressed for a long time afterwards. And this month it all came flooding back, as it was at this time of the year when the accident happened."

"My dear Watson, I am so sorry. Had I known I would not have asked you to read that letter."

"My dear fellow, there is nothing to apologise for. You could not have known."

Holmes could not shake his sense of guilt over the incident.

"Nevertheless, Watson, I hurt you by asking. Please accept my sincerest apologies."

Watson replied abruptly,

"Holmes, listen to me, this is not your fault, don't ever apologise for this. I need to work this out for myself, but just talking to you and having your presence here does help and I do appreciate it."

Holmes smiled; it was so like Watson to think of others before himself.

"Watson, if you need me, I'll be downstairs in the sitting room."

"Thank you, Holmes, I would rather like some time to myself. I'll see you in the morning, and I do appreciate you being here."

Holmes stood up and looked at Watson once more. He had got to the heart of the problem, but he was not convinced that Watson was recovered emotionally. Holmes decided to turn down the railway case. He had a more important case on his mind which took priority over everything else. He would do everything in his power to help Watson get through this difficult period.

"Good night, Watson."

"Good night, Holmes, and thank you."

Holmes left the room and closed the door behind him. Watson stood up and stretched and looked at the parcels on his bed. He would not be able to sleep tonight. Watson decided to start working on his model boat. He unwrapped the parcels and opened the box with the picture of the French Naval Vessel. The shipbuilding had begun.

Chapter Four: Launching The Boat

For several days, Watson spent much of his time in his room focusing on the naval project he had embarked upon. He did, however, make certain to spend some time with Holmes. Holmes, on his part, had been warm and welcoming. He had even asked Watson to join him for a walk on a few occasions, which Watson had to regretfully decline on account of his aching leg. Holmes accepted that, seeing Watson's discomfort. However Watson did accept an offer to venture out one night to a violin concert and he was totally mesmerised by it, much to Holmes's pleasure, who was both relieved and delighted to see Watson smiling and laughing once more. On returning from the concert hall, Holmes did have to offer Watson support as he struggled to walk; his leg had tired easily on this short trip.

As the days progressed, Watson found that his leg was slowly recovering, but he was running out of medical supplies to treat himself. He decided that he should now be able to cope walking by himself to the nearest chemist's, just a short stroll down Baker Street. Watson looked down at the model boat. The boat was almost finished, he just needed to   raise the flag and add some finishing touches to the sails. Watson smiled. He had found the combination of building the boat and enjoying Holmes's company to be very therapeutic and it was helping him overcome memories of his past. *Not exactly a ship in a bottle,* thought Watson, *but I hope Father would have been proud of it.* Tonight was Christmas Eve. As was their tradition, Holmes and Watson would exchange gifts at midnight. Watson looked forward to giving Holmes his Christmas present. It had also been a tradition in the Watson household to give a boat as a present to a relative or someone you loved. Watson had no one like that, but he did think of Holmes as a brother and he was proud to be able to combine the tradition with Christmas giving as well.

Watson put on his coat and walked down to the living room and smiled at Mrs Hudson, who began making her way upstairs. Watson put his head round the door to the living room and searched for Holmes. The room was filled with a dense smoky fog and Watson coughed. No doubt Holmes was here, somewhere!

"Holmes, I'm going out for a short walk, I think my leg is up to it, do you want to join me?"

There was no reply.

"Holmes?" asked Watson again after no response was forthcoming.

Holmes had been in his bedroom, having laid down his pipe. He had been out earlier that morning Christmas shopping and was just putting the finishing touches to Watson's present when he heard Watson calling out for him. Holmes got up and went into the living room and saw Watson with his head round the door.

"Yes, Watson, what is it?" said Holmes with a hint of irritability at Watson's unfortunate timing.

Surprised by Holmes's irritated response, Watson nonetheless replied calmly,

"Holmes, I'm just going out, would you care to join me? I'm only going just up Baker Street to get some medical supplies from the chemist's."

Holmes looked at Watson's smiling, eager face. He knew how much Watson enjoyed Christmas Eve and Holmes realised that Christmas Eve was not the same without his friend to share in the celebrations. He looked out of the window and saw the snow falling somewhat heavily. He could not risk Watson going out alone so soon after his leg had healed.

"All right, Watson, I'll get my coat," said Holmes, his lips curled into a half smile which vanished as quickly as it had appeared.

Watson's eyes twinkled with delight as Holmes accepted his offer of a walk. He had spent so much time on his own; it would be good to enjoy Holmes's company once more.

Holmes and Watson left their Baker Street flat and felt the chill of the winter air and the snowflakes falling down on them. Holmes wrapped his scarf round him in an effort to keep out the cold. Watson was at his side and he noticed that his leg though much improved was still not completely healed as there was a slight limp which troubled him. Holmes resolved to stay close to Watson. They had not been walking for long and were now at an enclosed square, a small pocket of green terrace in a city full of bricks and mortar.

"Holmes look up ahead, there is a band playing. *Good King Wenceslas*, if I hear correctly," said Watson jovially, interrupting Holmes's train of thought.

Holmes smiled at Watson. Watson looked happier than he had been in weeks and Holmes was heartened to see his Boswell smiling once more.

"Come then, Watson, let's go and hear them play", said Holmes as he slipped his arm in Watson's and proceeded to walk in the direction of the band.

Holmes and Watson stood listening to the band for almost an hour, enjoying the music. Watson had even participated in the singing of Christmas carols with the crowd. Holmes was simply content to watch and observe, but even he smiled and his eyes twinkled. For a moment in time, he could forget the world of crime and the criminal activity that thrived in London and enjoy the rare moment of seeing people united in celebration on Christmas Eve. Watson looked at Holmes and smiled. Earlier, Watson had bought some hot roasted chestnuts from a nearby stall and to his delight Holmes enjoyed the seasonal treat with him. He wrapped his heavy overcoat round him and grimaced as his leg began to throb again, he tried to ignore the pain shooting up his leg, not wanting this rare moment of peacefulness to end. But it gradually got worse and Watson's discomfort had not gone unobserved by

Holmes who caught Watson just as his leg began to give way.

"Watson!" cried Holmes with concern and immediately guided Watson to a nearby bench.

"I'm sorry Holmes, I was standing for far too long," replied Watson who strived to keep the embarrassment out of his voice.
Holmes sat beside Watson with his hand on Watson's shoulder.

"It's all right old fellow, it was not your fault, I should have realised how fast time has gone. Stay here, I'll go to the chemist and get you those medical supplies, as you need to rest that leg. I won't be long."

Watson nodded and thanked Holmes. He watched Holmes get up and walk away from him leaving the park and back into the street, heading toward the chemist. Watson smiled and leant back against the park bench, watching children throwing snowballs at each other and laughing. He closed his eyes for a few moments, trying to block out the pain in his aching leg, which was hurting him more than he had admitted to Holmes. Something wet and cold jolted Watson awake and he looked round in confusion. Then he looked down at his scarf and coat and noticed that they were covered in the remnants of a snowball that had clearly gone astray. Watson laughed as he saw a child aged no more than ten look at him fearfully.

"I'm sorry, sir, I did not mean to hit you."

"It's all right, lad, I can see it was an accident, go back and play with the others."

The boy's face lit up and he replied,

"Oh, thank you sir, Merry Christmas, sir!"

The boy scampered off and Watson smiled. He looked at his pocket watch and frowned. Holmes had been gone almost half an hour and he became concerned. It would be getting dark soon. Watson leant heavily on the arm of the bench and raised himself up struggling to do so and in some considerable pain. He staggered forward and was dismayed to realise that his leg was causing him considerable difficulty. Watson managed to walk to the street before leaning heavily against a street lamp, his breathing becoming more laboured. And then Watson heard a familiar voice calling out his name. He looked up to see a pair of grey eyes examining him closely.

"Watson, you should not be walking by yourself, you will do yourself an injury."

Before Watson could respond, Holmes slipped his arm around Watson's waist, supporting him as they began to walk down Baker Street back to their flat. Watson was grateful for this and leant heavily against Holmes.

"Thank you, Holmes," said Watson as they reached their front door.

They went inside the flat and walked slowly up the stairs and into the living room. Holmes guided Watson into his chair and stoked up the fire. He put the medical supplies down on the table and unwrapped a sachet of pain reliever which he mixed into a glass of water which Watson gratefully accepted. Holmes sat opposite him in his chair and for a long while they both sat silently looking at the blazing fire each lost in their own thoughts. The silence was interrupted by Mrs Hudson who had opened the door and was walking toward the dining table with a huge tray which she promptly set down.

"I took the liberty of preparing Christmas dinner, gentlemen, and once you have finished it, I will bring you both up some mulled wine seeing it is Christmas after all."

Holmes laughed and his eyes shone brightly replying "Thank you, Mrs Hudson, you are without a doubt the best landlady in London."

Holmes dashed into his bedroom and brought out a wrapped parcel which he gave to Mrs Hudson, saying playfully,

"Compliments of the season, Mrs Hudson."

Mrs Hudson blushed and unwrapped the parcel to find a patterned royal blue silk scarf. A hint of tears in her eyes, Mrs Hudson smiled and thanked Holmes before leaving the room.

Watson had been watching the scene between Holmes and the landlady. He never really would get Holmes's limits. Occasionally, Holmes revealed a great heart as well as a great mind. Watson slowly raised himself from his chair and stood up, leaning against the mantelpiece. The pain in his leg had subsided but it was still somewhat stiff. Watson slowly made his way to the dining table and sat down heavily in his chair.

Holmes eyed Watson with concern but said nothing, not wanting to hurt Watson's pride.

"Holmes, thank you for coming out today. I enjoyed it immensely despite the cold."

Holmes gave one of his rare smiles and replied,

"So did I, Watson, thank you for having me along."

They both continued talking, enjoying the meal and returning to their armchairs near the cozy warmth of the fire afterwards. Holmes picked up his violin and played pieces from Bach, Beethoven, and Mozart. Watson watched Holmes play and sat back, enjoying the moment and knowing he could not ask for anything more.
The clock struck midnight just as Holmes had finished playing his violin. He laid the instrument down and faced Watson.

"Merry Christmas, Watson," said Holmes as he picked up his glass and raised it.

Watson smiled, picked up his glass and raised it to meet Holmes's glass. The soft sound of the two glasses clinking echoed around the room.

Holmes vacated his seat and went into his bedroom. Watson did the same and limped toward the door.

"Back in a moment, Holmes!" cried Watson in Holmes's direction.

Watson heard Holmes's muttered "all right" and closed the door behind hum, slowly limping upstairs. He finally reached his room and saw the model boat just as he had left it that morning. Smiling, Watson picked up the tiny French flag and glued it onto the flagpole on the model boat. He hoped Holmes would like his Christmas present. He placed the boat inside the box, together with a card he had written the day before, and tied the box with a simple silk red ribbon. Watson left his bedroom, carefully carrying the box under his arm, leaving his other hand free to lean on the banister as he made his way back down the stairs. He leant heavily against the banister and was surprised to see Holmes open the door.

"Watson, you should have called for me if you were finding the stairs a struggle. You should sleep on the settee tonight; the stairs to your bedroom will be too much for you."

Watson was about to protest but then realised there was no escaping the truth of what Holmes had said. He *was* tired. Watson placed Holmes's present on the dining room table and allowed Holmes to help him to the couch. He placed both legs on the couch and sat propped up against the cushions. Holmes was sitting in his chair opposite him, stuffing his pipe with tobacco from his Persian slipper. He lit the pipe, and then bent down to reach for a parcel which he gave to Watson.

"Merry Christmas, Watson!"

Watson opened up his parcel and when he had finished unwrapping it, his eyes widened in astonishment. He gripped the soft leather medical bag and saw *Dr J H Watson* embossed at the top centre. It was a somewhat expensive medical bag he had been anxious to get, as his old medical bag was becoming worn. Quite a number of times, he had stared at it longingly through the window of the shop selling medical supplies and other equipment.

"Holmes, how did you guess?!"

Holmes laughed in delight at Watson's astonishment.

"It took no great deduction to observe your old medical bag was looking worn out after many years of use. I also know you have been cutting down on spending of late, spending less time playing billiards at the club, and I have been with you once or twice when we passed the shop when visiting Charing Cross Hospital on business. These were all the clues I needed to know what you wanted."

Watson looked at Holmes fondly and whispered softly,

"Thank you Holmes, it is most generous and thoughtful of you."

Holmes smiled,

"If you look inside the bag, Watson, you will find one more surprise!"

Watson undid the latch on the medical bag and peered inside. He laughed as he pulled out a box of cigars and a small flask of brandy.

"Not what you would normally find in a medical bag, but I trust you will enjoy the Sherlock Holmes prescription!"

Both men laughed heartily and then Watson spluttered through his laughter,
"Holmes, your present is on the table. I'm afraid I can't get up to give it to you, I'm sorry."

Holmes got up and brought the box back to where they were sitting. He undid the bow, lifted the box lid off, and looked inside. He caught his breath as he saw the object inside the box; carefully, he lifted it out and stared at it in astonishment.

"Watson, did you make this? It's marvelous!"

Watson smiled as he saw Sherlock Holmes genuinely astonished by what he was holding in his hand.

"Yes, I did, Holmes. You see, it was a tradition in the Watson household for the gift of a ship in a bottle to be given to other members of the family. Before my father was killed, one of the last things we did together was to make a ship in a bottle which I still have today. Well, I have never had the opportunity to make one for anyone else, and so I made you this boat. I hope you like it, Holmes."

His eyes glistening, Holmes looked up at Watson.

"Watson, thank you. I am truly touched by what you have given me and will place this wonderful boat by my bedside so as to see it every morning when I wake up."

Watson smiled; he felt truly happy. He drained his glass of mulled wine and settled back against his cushions, watching Holmes. He was exhausted; it had been a long day, *but very much a fulfilling one*, thought Watson as he watched Holmes carefully place his wooden boat down and proceeded to open the card that accompanied the boat. He felt his eyes get heavier and heavier as he watched Holmes.

Holmes opened up the card which Watson had given him which read simply

To Holmes,
What is a friend? A single soul in two bodies.
- Aristotle
 Holmes, my friend and brother, Merry Christmas
Watson

Holmes looked up and started to call out Watson's name but stopped short as he saw that Watson was asleep, a smile of contentment on his face. Holmes stood up quietly, took his boat into his bedroom, placed it carefully on his bookcase, then took an afghan rug from his wardrobe, came back into the sitting room, and placed it gently over the sleeping form. He looked at Watson for a long while and then smiled affectionately, sitting down back in his chair opposite him.

"I consider you my brother, too, my dear fellow," Holmes said softly.

He looked at Watson once more before turning back to look at the fire and then settled back in his chair, allowing sleep to wash over him. Outside, the snow started falling once more and in the street below a small choir gathered in the street singing *Silent Night*. London was at peace. But it was not the music that permeated the flat of 221B Baker Street; instead it was the silence of friendship and brotherhood that filled the flat that Christmas morning. A friendship that would sail on the oceans of time forever.

Also from MX Publishing

Close To Holmes

A Look at the Connections Between Historical London, Sherlock Holmes and Sir Arthur Conan Doyle.

Eliminate The Impossible

An Examination of the World of Sherlock Holmes on Page and Screen.

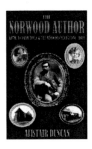

The Norwood Author

Arthur Conan Doyle and the Norwood Years (1891 - 1894) – Winner of the 2011 Howlett Literary Award (Sherlock Holmes book of the year)

www.mxpublishing.com

Also From MX Publishing

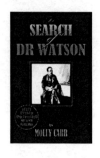

In Search of Dr Watson

Wonderful biography of Dr. Watson from expert Molly Carr – 2nd edition fully updated.

Arthur Conan Doyle, Sherlock Holmes and Devon

A Complete Tour Guide and Companion.

The Lost Stories of Sherlock Holmes

Eight more stories from the pen of John H Watson – compiled by Tony Reynolds.

www.mxpublishing.com

Also From MX Publishing

Watsons Afghan Adventure

Fascinating biography of Watson's time in Afghanistan from US Army veteran Kieran McMullen.

Shadowfall

Sherlock Holmes, ancient relics and demons and mystic characters. A supernatural Holmes pastiche.

Official Papers of The Hound of The Baskervilles

Very unusual collection of the original police papers from The Hound case.

www.mxpublishing.com

Also From MX Publishing

The Sign of Fear

The first adventure of the 'female Sherlock Holmes'. A delightful fun adventure with your favourite supporting Holmes characters.

A Study in Crimson

The second adventure of the 'female Sherlock Holmes' with a host of sub-plots and new characters joining Watson and Fanshaw

The Chronology of Arthur Conan Doyle

The definitive chronology used by historians and libraries worldwide.

www.mxpublishing.com

Also From MX Publishing

The Outstanding Mysteries of
Sherlock Holmes

With thirteen Homes stories and
illustrations Kelly re-creates the
gas-lit, fog-enshrouded world of
Victorian London

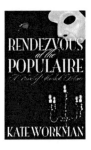

Rendezvous at The Populaire

Sherlock Holmes has retired,
injured from an encounter with
Moriarty. He's tempted out of
retirement for an epic battle with
the Phantom of the opera.

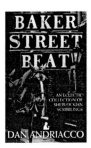

Baker Street Beat

An eclectic collection of articles,
essays, radio plays and 'general
scribblings' about Sherlock Holmes
from Dr.Dan Andriacco.

www.mxpublishing.com

Also From MX Publishing

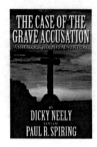

The Case of The Grave Accusation

The creator of Sherlock Holmes has been accused of murder. Only Holmes and Watson can stop the destruction of the Holmes legacy.

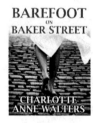

Barefoot on Baker Street

Epic novel of the life of a Victorian workhouse orphan featuring Sherlock Holmes and Moriarty.

Case of Witchcraft

A tale of witchcraft in the Northern Isles, in which long-concealed secrets are revealed -- including some that concern the Great Detective himself!

www.mxpublishing.com

Also From MX Publishing

The Affair In Transylvania

Holmes and Watson tackle Dracula in deepest Transylvania in this stunning adaptation by film director Gerry O'Hara

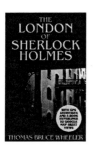

The London of Sherlock Holmes

400 locations including GPS co-ordinates that enable Google Street view of the locations around London in all the Homes stories

I Will Find The Answer

Sequel to Rendezvous At The Populaire, Holmes and Watson tackle Dr.Jekyll.

www.mxpublishing.com

Also From MX Publishing

The Case of The Russian Chessboard

Short novel covering the dark world of Russian espionage sees Holmes and Watson on the world stage facing dark and complex enemies.

An Entirely New Country

Covers Arthur Conan Doyle's years at Undershaw where he wrote Hound of The Baskervilles. Foreword by Mark Gatiss (BBC's Sherlock).

Shadowblood

Sequel to Shadowfall, Holmes and Watson tackle blood magic, the vilest form of sorcery.

www.mxpublishing.com

Also From MX Publishing

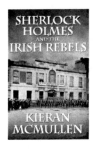

Sherlock Holmes and The Irish Rebels

It is early 1916 and the world is at war. Sherlock Holmes is well into his spy persona as Altamont.

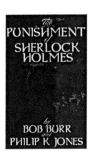

The Punishment of Sherlock Holmes

"deliberately and successfully funny"

The Sherlock Holmes Society of London

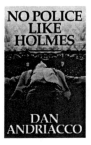

No Police Like Holmes

It's a Sherlock Holmes symposium, and murder is involved. The first case for Sebastian McCabe.

www.mxpublishing.com

Also From MX Publishing

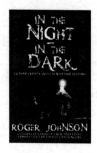

In The Night, In The Dark

Winner of the Dracula Society Award – a collection of supernatural ghost stories from the editor of the Sherlock Holmes Society of London journal.

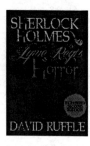

Sherlock Holmes and The Lyme Regis Horror

Fully updated 2nd edition of this bestselling Holmes story set in Dorset.

My Dear Watson

Winner of the Suntory Mystery Award for fiction and translated from the original Japanese. Holmes greatest secret is revealed – Sherlock Holmes is a woman.

www.mxpublishing.com

Also From MX Publishing

Mark of The Baskerville Hound

100 years on and a New York policeman faces a similar terror to the great detective.

A Professor Reflects On Sherlock Holmes

A wonderful collection of essays and scripts and writings on Sherlock Holmes.

Sherlock Holmes On The Air

A collection of Sherlock Holmes radio scripts with detailed notes on Canonical references.

www.mxpublishing.com

Also From MX Publishing

Sherlock Holmes Whos Who

All the characters from the entire canon catalogued and profiled.

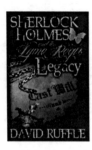

Sherlock Holmes and The Lyme Regis Legacy

Sequel to the Lyme Regis Horror and Holmes and Watson are once again embroiled in murder in Dorset.

Sherlock Holmes and The Discarded Cigarette

London 1895. A well known author, a theoretical invention made real and the perfect crime.

Also From MX Publishing

Sherlock Holmes and The Whitechapel Vampire

Jack The Ripper is a vampire, and Holmes refusal to believe it could lead to his downfall.

Tales From The Strangers Room

A collection of writings from more than 20 Sherlockians with author profits going to The Beacon Society.

The Secret Journal of Dr Watson

Holmes and Watson head to the newly formed Soviet Union to rescue the Romanovs.

www.mxpublishing.com

Lightning Source UK Ltd.
Milton Keynes UK
UKOW041118210612

194818UK00006B/29/P